Chase was there. Leaning against the front of her little SUV, arms crossed casually over his chest as he watched her approach.

"What are you doing here?" she demanded.

But he shook his head, staring at her curiously. "The question is this—what the hell do you think you're doing?"

She angled her head and narrowed her eyes. "I'm taking my dad's place. Just like you're sitting in for Hank—"

"I've sat in before. You've avoided the band like it's the plague."

"I've changed my mind."

He walked over to her, not touching her, just standing a few bare inches from her. "I know you," he said softly. "And I know how you felt about your father. I don't know what you're up to, but I do know this—you've got to be careful, Sky."

"I'm not up to anything. Why should I be careful? My dad died because of a tragic accident, right?"

"Please, be careful."

A MURDERER AMONG US

NEW YORK TIMES BESTSELLING AUTHOR

HEATHER GRAHAM

INTRIGUE

In loving memory of my mom. Born in Ireland, she embraced her new country, became a copy editor for an ad company and was my first before-I-dared-send-it-out editor. Strong, fierce and kind—but mostly fierce, when it came to the English language!

Recycling programs for this product may not exist in your area.

ISBN-13: 978-1-335-45678-6

A Murderer Among Us

Harlequin Enterprises ULC
22 Adelaide St. West, 41st Floor
Toronto, Ontario M5H 4E3, Canada
www.Harlequin.com

Printed in U.S.A.

New York Times and *USA TODAY* bestselling author **Heather Graham** has written more than two hundred novels. She is pleased to have been published in over twenty-five languages, with sixty million books in print. Heather is a proud recipient of the Silver Bullet from Thriller Writers and was awarded the prestigious Thriller Master Award in 2016. She is also a recipient of Lifetime Achievement Awards from RWA and *The Strand* and is the founder of The Slush Pile Players, an author band and theatrical group. An avid scuba diver, ballroom dancer and mother of five, she still enjoys her South Florida home but also loves to travel. Heather is grateful every day for a career she loves so very much.

For more information, check out her website, theoriginalheathergraham.com, or find Heather on Facebook.

Books by Heather Graham

Harlequin Intrigue

Undercover Connection
Out of the Darkness
Shadows in the Night
Law and Disorder
Tangled Threat
A Murderer Among Us

Visit the Author Profile page at Harlequin.com.

CAST OF CHARACTERS

Skylar "Sky" Ferguson—Daughter of Jake Ferguson. When Sky agrees to take her father's place in Skyhawk's "reunion" gig in 2024, she's also looking for answers...and soon plummets into an old world of evil and deceit.

Chase McCoy—An old flame of Skylar's, the FBI agent and grandson of Hank McCoy is seeking the truth of the past as well. But will he and Skylar rekindle the fire that raged between them as they risk everything together?

Jake Ferguson—Father of Skylar. A Vietnam veteran, Jake was the lead guitarist and vocalist of the band Skyhawk until 2017, when he died onstage under mysterious circumstances...

Hank McCoy—Original drummer for Skyhawk and Chase's grandfather.

Skyhawk—Legendary band fronted by Jake Ferguson and formed in 1974. Their third album went platinum in 1980. Original members included Chris Wiley (bass), Joe Garcia (keyboards) and Mark Reynolds (rhythm guitar), along with Ferguson and McCoy.

Charlie Bentley, Justin West and Nathan Harrison—Regular roadies for Skyhawk over the years.

Kenneth Malcolm—Manager of the hometown arena where Skyhawk are set to play their "reunion" gig, with Skylar and Chase standing in for their famous relatives.

Prologue

1949

"Oh! He kicks and punches and—" Cindy Ferguson broke off with a gasp and a shriek "—he's either a football player or a soccer star!" she finished. She shrugged through the pain and said softly, "Or a rock star, like his dad! You know, you're supposed to be doing studio work right now—"

"Hardly a rock star—just a studio musician. There are other studio musicians," Aidan Ferguson assured her. "This kid has one mom—and one dad. I'm a so-so musician. I intend to be a great dad!"

"You're already a great husband," Cindy assured him. "And don't kid yourself, a great musician. You could play with so many groups, but you stay with me!"

"Pain meds are making me look good," Aidan teased.

"If only I had some pain meds!"

Her water had broken; they'd rushed into the ER and were assured her doctor would be right there.

Aidan watched his wife in distress, trying to return her smile. He reminded himself that childbirth was a natural event.

The pain that came with it was natural, too. Cindy would be fine.

But he was worried. They had come to the hospital too late. Cindy was already in heavy labor, fighting the pain. The nurse had been in, but along with his worrying, he was growing nervous and angry—where the hell was the doctor?

As if on cue, Dr. Jamison walked in, wasting no time on small talk. He gave Cindy a lightning-quick examination and shouted, "Delivery room. Now!"

Cindy was whisked out.

Aidan was left to pace the room until a nurse showed him out and into the waiting room where it seemed he joined a cavalcade of marchers: fathers, others, just pacing in circles as they awaited news of the births of their children. He thought about how his phone was probably ringing: his world was a good one, and even though he was just a studio musician he knew that big names would be calling to congratulate him. That made him smile, and, of course, thinking about them helped make the time go by. And he'd been warned that even now, it could be a while.

He was stunned when the doctor who had so recently left with his wife appeared again almost immediately.

"Mr. Ferguson?"

"Yes, yes!" Aidan wasn't sure why the mere mention of his name frightened him so much. He didn't mean to be a pessimist. But…

"Something happened, something is wrong!" he said anxiously, reaching the doctor.

"Uh, no, Mr. Ferguson. They're seeing to your wife and child now. A little boy, sir. Or, should I say, a big boy. He's ten pounds one ounce. Mother and son are doing fine. You'll be able to see them soon."

Aidan thought he muttered a thanks—he wasn't even

sure. He sank into one of the chairs, his head falling into his hands.

Ten pounds. Kind of giant for a newborn? A boy. Every dad's dream, ten pounds, big and strong, maybe he was going to be a star football player!

In thirty minutes, he was allowed to see Cindy and his newborn son.

And the baby was beautiful. He looked as if he was a few weeks old already, as if he could walk out of his bassinet. He had a full head of dark hair.

He kissed his wife, shaking his head as he sat next to her, stroking her hair, leaning over to give her a gentle kiss. "Thank you, thank you," he told her. The emotion welling in him was almost unbearable.

"Thank you, Dad," she teased. "I couldn't have done it alone."

He grinned. "Well, you had the hard part."

"No, actually, you had the *hard* part!" she teased.

A nurse cleared her throat from the doorway and they both looked up, reddening.

"Um, sorry. I have papers here. Have you thought about a name yet?" she asked.

Aidan looked at his wife. She smiled. "Jake. For your dad," she said.

"Jake. For my dad," he agreed. And nurse or no nurse, he leaned over to kiss her again.

"Thank you. That boy is like…my life!"

"He is *our* lives," she corrected. "Our beautiful boy."

Jake Mallory Ferguson *did* become their lives. Cindy Ferguson was diagnosed with cervical cancer a year later; her life was saved, but their son was to be their only child.

And for years, he was their beautiful, beautiful boy. He

had a thick thatch of dark hair, amazing, riveting blue eyes and a smile that could charm the coldest heart.

Through grade and middle schools, he was a wonderful student, popular *and* smart.

He did play football, even through his senior year, when he found two things: that he loved the guitar, which was great, and drugs—not so great.

In fact, the alcohol and drugs had gotten so bad that when he graduated, he knew his father was going to let him be drafted.

Aidan and Cindy were deeply distressed. A neighborhood boy had already been killed in Vietnam.

But a neighborhood girl had already died of an overdose as well.

And all their efforts, punishments, encouragements to get help…all had done nothing.

Aidan had served in World War II himself. Jake had been born as part of the baby boom that had come when the war had finally ended. Aidan had seen bad action: he knew the price of war. And he knew, too, he was still glad he had fought, that he had been privileged to help liberate one of the concentration camps.

And so, when Jake came to his father, begging for the money so he could opt out of college, Aidan hesitated just briefly in agony before giving his answer.

"Son, if you're going to kill yourself, you might as well do so for your country."

Of course, Jake hated him. But he went off and enlisted in the navy before he could be ordered into a different branch of the service.

And in the service, he found help rather than death. He found others who had suffered from his same addictions and an organization that helped in a way no lecture or punishment could.

He still loved his guitar. And when he emerged from the service, he decided to make it his focus.

A truly beautiful boy. And in time, well, in time he became something Aidan had never imagined for his son. Something wonderful, and scary, of course.

He followed his dad into music.

But he didn't become a studio musician.

He somehow became a rock star.

Amazing. Terrifying.

But the lifestyle didn't alter the joy he had learned with his group in the navy, it just put him in a great position to write songs, to handle the band's business, to live… wonderfully.

He bought his parents a great new house in Palm Beach with a heated pool and a Jacuzzi. He lived down the street.

But Aidan continued to worry as the years passed.

Not because Jake fell back—miraculously, he never did. But neither did he fall in love. Oh, well, of course there were women in his life. Some stayed a while. But it seemed he was never really going to fall in love.

He'd never know what Aidan and Cindy had now been sharing all these years, through World War II, Korea, the sixties—being kind of flower children—the seventies, tragedy in the country, days of peace, days of faith…

The eighties, when Jake's band became about the biggest thing in history—well, after the Beatles, the Rolling Stones, and a few others—maybe.

The nineties, the Gulf Wars…

And then, a bit before the millennium…

It was only then, when Jake Ferguson was about to turn

fifty, that he found the love of his life. He and his group had been playing at Madison Square Garden and she had been with the backup singers for their opening group. They'd gone for coffee together, and in the days to come, they went to the Met, to the Museum of Natural History, for long walks in the park, to the zoo, to the theater...

He brought her home to Florida and announced to his parents he was going to be married at last. Her name was Mandy Mannix, and she wasn't as old as Jake, but she was a respectable thirty-eight. They teased Aidan and Cindy about heading to Vegas to be married by an Elvis impersonator, but they were married at the church the family had gone to forever, even if it was a quiet affair for their families and closest friends. Jake hadn't wanted a media frenzy.

He went on to write, play and perform with his band—with Mandy singing backup for his group, Skyhawk.

Then something that seemed miraculous happened. Jake and Mandy had their own baby.

A little girl, a beautiful little girl with dark hair and stunning blue eyes. Because of those eyes, and partially because of the name of Jake's band as well, the baby was named Skylar and called Sky. Sometimes, Sky Blue.

She became everyone's life, and Aidan was beyond grateful both he and Cindy were still alive and well—old as dirt, but alive and well—to see the birth of that baby. They both got to see her first toddling steps, hear her first words, hear themselves called Nana and Papa.

They both made it until their loving little granddaughter arrived at her fifth birthday.

Then, in Aidan's arms, Cindy passed away, whispering her last words.

"I love you."

He knew that he would follow her soon enough. In return Aidan whispered, "I will find you in clouds of peace and beauty."

It was another six years before Aidan was to join her.

And while it broke Skylar's heart to see her beloved grandfather die, she was almost grateful after another six years had passed because he didn't have to witness what happened.

Because then, she lost her beloved father…

His father would have been devastated by the way it all happened.

When she received the strange call seven years after his death, she was reminded. And she was as angry as she had been devastated and determined that she would find out what had really happened, and she would clear his name for the ages.

Jake Ferguson had been an incredible man. A legend, a rock legend, and yet a wise man who had turned his life around and become an amazing human being as well. And he deserved to be remembered in all the best ways.

So…

Yes.

She would join Skyhawk for a special anniversary performance.

She would take her father's place.

And maybe, just maybe, she could figure out what the hell had really happened.

Chapter One

2024

“Hey, our guys are young in comparison to a few of them out there!”

Sky smiled as she listened to Brandon Wiley, five years her senior and the son of Chris Wiley, bass guitarist for Skyhawk—not quite as late of a bloomer as her father. “Come on, now. My dad wasn’t even twenty when they put the band together,” Brandon continued. “He’s a mere sixty-nine!”

“And I take nothing away from your dad, for sure!” Sky promised. “He’s an incredible performer. And I’m betting that my dad still would have been incredible, even at seventy-five!”

“Agreed. Hey, Mick Jagger is over eighty and I saw one of his performances last year—the dude still rules the stage,” Brandon said. He paused, looking down. “Sky, I’m so sorry about your dad—”

“Thank you. I know.” Her smile was a constricted one. “And my mother would have insisted on an autopsy, even if the supposedly accidental death hadn’t called for one. There were no drugs in my father’s system. What happened was—”

"Truly a tragic accident," Brandon said quickly. "We all know that. And, of course, we went over and over it all when it happened, and I didn't say that to dredge up the past."

They stood in the studio in the New Orleans Central Business District where Skyhawk had recorded their first album. Sky turned, wincing, because on the wall, there was a picture of the original band members of Skyhawk: her father, Jake Ferguson, vocalist and lead guitar; Brandon's dad, Chris Wiley, bassist; Joe Garcia, keyboards; Mark Reynolds, rhythm guitar; and Hank McCoy, drummer.

Her dad—at the ripe old age of twenty-five when he'd started the band—had been the oldest in the group. And it was true—compared to some of the rockers still dancing their hearts out on stage, the remaining members of Skyhawk were just in their sixties. Back from the service and freshly graduated, her dad had been asked for help from Hank McCoy, a neighbor, and in helping out someone he saw as a little brother, Jake had wound up creating Skyhawk.

And the remaining members of the group could still rock the house—now sometimes with the help of children and grandchildren.

Sky had been asked to join with the group before. The band was still getting gigs—good ones. But not the instantly sold-out gigs they'd gotten when her father was alive.

For years, she'd politely refused any interaction with the group. Her mother had remained close friends with many of them and their assorted wives, ex-wives and children. But the publicity surrounding her father's death still plagued her.

He'd been electrocuted by a faulty amp. The accident had been deemed *user error.*

She had never believed it. Her father had known how to set a stage, but, of course, once Skyhawk had gotten big—and then huge—they had roadies to handle all of that for them. But something had been wrong that night, and Jake Ferguson had gone to check the amp and…boom. Electricity had crackled, and the explosion of the equipment and the ensuing fire that might have engulfed the entire place had taken his life.

Drugs had immediately been suspected, and headlines had read different versions of *Did Ferguson Crack after Nearly 50 Years of Clean Living?*

She'd been furious, of course. And the autopsy had served them well: no, he had been clean as a whistle.

Accident. It had been a tragic accident.

Somehow, though, Sky couldn't accept it. The part of her who had adored the man who had received such adulation and still been the best husband and dad in the world argued that there had to have been something amiss. Her logical self argued that even if there had been something off, there would be no way she could discover what it was this long after the fact. Because while the facts of his death had gotten out, she knew there were many among his fans and his doubters who were convinced it had all been a cover-up.

"Sky."

She was startled to hear her name spoken softly in a deep, rich and quiet voice. Swinging around, she saw that Chase McCoy, the grandson of the drummer, had arrived.

She winced. She'd been eighteen, Chase twenty-one, when they'd fallen into a wild crush. Life had been fun then. She had just entered college, following in her parents' footsteps, majoring in music. Chase, three years her senior, had been sitting in for Hank, playing drums for several of the gigs, making his own name. Her dad had brought her on stage for a ballad he had written, a song that still commanded the airwaves, as well as several music platforms.

And Chase…

Well, she'd been eighteen, and a pretty typical eighteen. Bursting into adulthood with tremendous excitement. She had the most loving and supportive parents in the world, wise beyond their years, parents who had seriously taught her the dangers of excess and more.

Somehow, they hadn't prepared her for Chase.

First, of course, at that age, she had gone for the physical. Chase was simply striking. A solid six three of lean muscle with dark auburn hair and hazel eyes that could burn like crystals. He could play, and he had a voice that lent incredibly to Skyhawk songs and backup vocals. Jake Ferguson had loved him and his talent and had been writing a song especially for him when…

When the accident had occurred.

And at that point, she'd backed away from the band and, to the best of her ability, anyone associated with it.

She'd heard that Chase was now doing much more than music. While many thought that garage-band talent was instinctive and natural, both Hank and her dad had believed in higher education, and while Chase had also continued his music studies, she understood that after her father's death, he had opted for a major in criminology, had graduated and was working in that field somewhere. She wasn't sure who he worked for or what he was doing.

Except now, of course, he was filling in on drums for

Hank, who had recently had heart surgery. Hank was going to be around, supervising and commenting, Sky was certain. But Chase would be the drummer for most of the numbers they were doing.

"Chase. Hey. How are you doing?" she asked, relieved her voice sounded completely casual. She still felt anything but casual regarding Chase.

But everything that had happened had been her fault.

That had been years ago now. They had both gone on. But there had been a time when they had lamented being the daughter of one rock star and the grandson of another.

Not as bad for him as it had been for her, Chase had always told her. The lead vocalist was always the front man, the name and face people knew. Those who just listened on the radio or bought the music knew the name of a group if they loved it, and after that, the name of the lead singer, and not so much the other members of the band.

She wondered now if that was still true. There had been so much publicity when her father had died. The media had hopped on it, interviewing band members, fans, producers…

She had managed to hide away. Mostly. Once upon a time, she'd recorded with her father. And that recording had hit the airwaves big-time.

Chase was studying her. She wondered if he was reading her mind.

"So, cool," she murmured. "I'm going to be my dad, and you're going to be your grandfather."

"And you are going to have to rehearse like hell," Brandon said dryly, grinning. "I've only been asked to sit in on a few numbers and some backup vocals. You two…

What is Skyhawk without the lead vocalist and a kick-ass drummer?"

"Well, here you go, Brandon. We grew up with these guys, with this music," Sky told him.

"She's right. I think I knew a lot of the Skyhawk lineup before I knew my ABCs," Chase told him. "So today is—" He broke off, looking around the studio. It was meant for recording, but today, they would be putting together the fivesome playing the main frame of the performance, Joe Garcia still on keyboards, Mark Reynolds still on rhythm guitar and Chris Wiley on bass—except on a few numbers where he wanted Brandon to sit in. "Today, we're just seeing how we do," Chase finished.

"Yeah. My dad and Mark and Joe should be here any minute," Brandon said. He looked at Sky. "Are you going to do your dad's ballad?" he asked quietly. "My dad said that you've turned them down every time they've asked you on stage, even to do the ballad."

Sky forced a smile and shrugged. "I don't know. You mean 'Grace,' I take it. My dad wrote several ballads."

"Yeah," Brandon said. "That one. Come on, kid, that video of you and your dad years ago is *still* viral. It could make this whole thing for everyone!"

"Maybe," she murmured.

"Hey," Chase said. "If it hurts you to do it—don't. But think about it. Maybe doing it in his memory will be good for...well, for you remembering the good times and... learning to go on despite what happened."

"I am going on!" she protested. Though, in truth, telling her that to do or not do the song was her decision was Chase standing up for her. "My dad has been dead years now, and I am a normal, functioning human being," she assured them both.

"Oh, yeah, of course!" Brandon said. "It's just that music is something you always loved so much—"

"And then again, define *normal*!" Chase teased.

Sky found she was laughing—*normally*. Chase had a way of saying things that made uneasy moments easy. Teasing, gently. And yet, when she looked at him, she thought she remembered enough about him to see that behind his banter, he was worried about her.

She forced another sweet smile.

"Let's face it, we're the family members of rock stars. No one expects us to be normal," she assured Chase. "And you! More than anyone. As amazing on the drums as your grandfather—and you stopped music to major in criminology. What? Have you decided to be a cop? May have to change your name for that, and unless you have major plastic surgery, you'll never be able to go undercover."

Chase shrugged. "I found out that I liked it, that it's fascinating."

"What? Ugh. Studying blood and guts?" Brandon asked.

"All kinds of cool stuff—not so much blood and guts," Chase countered. He shrugged. "I already had my arts and music degree, but I realized I find fingerprints, shoeprints, fibers and especially the psychology of crime to be fascinating. It is really amazing what profilers can come up with."

"And screw up with, too, right?"

"It's an inexact science, but right more often than not. It's not a be-all and end-all. It's a tool like dozens of the machines out there that can pinpoint where certain soil particles might have come from and where fabrics were made… Trust me, it's cool. Fun, intriguing," Chase said. "Anyway…"

The door to their rehearsal area opened and closed. Joe Garcia and Mark Reynolds had arrived.

"Sky!" Mark exclaimed, stepping forward to encompass her in a great hug.

She'd communicated with him—and Joe, Hank and Chris—through the years, politely refusing every time they'd asked her to join them.

She'd even seen them a few times: her mother had remained friends with everyone, grateful for their support, she had told Sky.

She'd never understood Sky's aversion to her father's people. And Sky couldn't explain to her mother that she just didn't trust any of them.

A therapist would tell her that she just couldn't accept the truth.

But that wouldn't cut it. They would never understand. She couldn't accept what she didn't believe to be truth. Her mother had tried so hard to help her, and for her mother's sake, she had pretended she was accepting her dad's death and moving on.

And as far as her father's band, well, it had been simpler just to go her own way.

But now…

"All right, then!" Joe Garcia announced, grinning. "Let's start with some of our hard rockin' tunes and go on from there. Everything is here: drums, keyboards, guitars and, most importantly, us! Let's get to it. Sky of Skyhawk!"

She smiled. She had always loved Joe. He was a good guy. The youngest in the group at a mere sixty-seven, he could pass for a man twenty years his junior. He had a rich headful of snow-white hair, worked out daily, she was sure, and looked more like a rugged action star than a musician. He had a keen sense of humor and, more importantly, a solid grip on life, reality and the simple fact that fame meant nothing if you didn't have your health and people to love. His wife, Josie, was one of Sky's mom's best friends. Joe and Josie had never had children of their own; instead, they had spent their time helping out at children's hospitals and seeing that those in areas devastated by wars, famine, fires and storms found the care they needed.

She reminded herself she believed someone here was guilty of being involved in her father's death.

But not Joe.

"I'm sitting in for my dad until he gets here," Brandon told them. "But I've done it before. Chase, you've actually sat in a few times, too. So… Sky. You ready for this?"

She smiled sweetly. "As ready as I'll ever be," she assured them.

Mark Reynolds, slim, wiry and with his own full head of snow-white hair, touched her gently on the shoulders.

"Your dad will be smiling from heaven," he said softly.

"Thanks for that. So…"

"Hey, Chase has been the drummer before, and you've played and sung for your dad before, and Brandon sits in, too, so it's just darned cool we're together and doing this. Think about it! Your dad would be seventy-five, and he created the band in the seventies, several decades of music. We're pretty darned…"

"Old?" Brandon suggested dryly.

"Hey!" Chris protested, glaring at his son when he arrived.

"Sorry, Dad!"

"Jagger is still older. Sir Paul McCartney is older! We're classic rock," Chris said.

"*Classic*, okay!" Brandon teased. "Come on, my fellow generationers," he begged. "Help me out here."

"Oh, hell no, you're on your own!" Chase teased.

"Right. Age is all in the mind, and you've got a young mind, right, Dad?"

"Yeah. The mind is still young. The knees—not so much. But when the music is going…I'm young at heart."

"Right. And whatever! Let's go. I've got a list. We'll start with 'Rock the World.' And go, go, go!" Mark said.

Chase slid onto the stool behind the drum set, Joe moved over to the keyboards, and the others picked up their instruments.

Sky knew the songs. She feared, though, that she'd be awkward, that her timing would be off…that something wouldn't be right.

But she moved her fingers over the opening chords and slid easily into one of Skyhawk's most popular songs.

"Rocking the world, in the best way, come on,

I say, let's make her the very best today.

There was a time my soul was sad, out there everything was bad,

in a world so bad, let's change the fad, it's time, it's time, it's time, today,

because *we* are the way.

In a world of troubles, we can hit a few doubles,

being the good

the way that we should.

Now my heart sings as I rock the world, rock the world, rock the rockin' world!"

FAST, WITH GREAT riffs and a drum solo, it was one of the songs that could just about wake the dead and cause the staidest human being to dance or, at the very least, wriggle in a chair to the music.

Chase killed the drum solo.

She picked up with the second verse, thinking of the person her father must have been back in 1974. He'd fallen into a horrible place but come back from it, even through war and the horror of seeing friends blown to bits. But he was determined, as he had once told her, that the more good done in the world, the less the bad could conquer.

She sang the second verse, and they held a long note before the drums slammed in for the crescendo.

And while Chris Wiley was playing his guitar, Brandon was at a mic for backup on the chorus refrains, and to Sky's surprise, the signature song went off without a hitch.

They were all silent.

"The rest of this can't possibly go so well," Joe Garcia said, shaking his head. "Wow."

"Onward," Mark said.

"Yeah, yeah, of course," Joe agreed.

"No, I meant 'Onward' is the next song on the list," Mark said dryly.

"Onward and onward," Sky said, surprised that, once again, her fingers moved over her father's guitar strings, and the words came swiftly to her lips.

There were a few snags, a few suggestions from one

band member to another, and a little reworking, but for the most part, they sailed through the rehearsal.

And they were shockingly good, in sync.

Sky found she was enjoying herself. Skyhawk songs, mostly written by her dad, perhaps didn't comprise the most brilliant lyrics known to man, but with the music that was catchy and almost magical, the pieces stood the rigors of time.

"Sky, ready?" Joe Garcia asked her.

She was startled. The ballad. They wanted her to do her father's ballad.

"Intro is the keyboard," she said. No way to put it off. And it was ridiculous. But it was the one song she had done at home with her father, sitting in the living room, talking about life. He wanted her to live her dreams, never his or her mother's, but *her* dreams. They didn't have to be musical dreams.

And she had assured him she didn't know what she wanted out of life—except to have a family as beautiful as the one he and her mom had created for her.

He'd hugged her. She'd asked him about his favorite song.

The ballad. "Dreams."

Keyboards, a gentle guitar entry, then the lyrics…

"Like the falcon soars to the skies
My heart is lifted with a magic like their wings,
For in the depth and beauty of your eyes
All that is me, deep in my soul, rises high
And sings.
There is magic, magic, in this thing I feel,
Magic, magic, my heart on fire
And I know that it is real."

Chase joined in on the chorus, his voice deep and rich. She was pleased at how wonderful he sounded and that it was oddly good while it hurt at the same time. She turned to glance at him as she sang. He was looking at her.

And she wasn't sure of what she saw in his eyes. Empathy? Strangely…worry.

"There is magic, oh so real, beauty in this thing I feel, my heart rises to skies,

For the magic in your eyes. Magic…magic…"

She almost missed the first beat of the second verse, but in the end, she finished the song—again with the chorus.

Again, with Chase McCoy.

She was stunned when the rest of the group applauded energetically. She turned to see Joe heading over to her, taking her into his arms in a warm hug.

"Oh, Sky, your dad would be so proud!" he exclaimed.

Mark said softly, "Tears in heaven, that was so… beautiful. You did him proud, kid."

Brandon and Chris Wiley echoed their congratulations.

"Skyhawk is going to soar!" Brandon added excitedly.

She thanked them all.

Only Chase hadn't spoken. He was still at his drum set. Watching her, that strange mix of empathy and concern in his eyes.

"Okay. So much for flattering ourselves!" Mark said. "Tomorrow afternoon at the arena, and the night after—showtime."

"And remember, we've been in a studio rehearsal space—next will be at the arena, and we all know that we have to adjust to the size of a location," Mark said.

"We'll have the crew there, too," Joe reminded him. "Setting up the amps for sound—"

He broke off awkwardly. There was silence.

"Guys, it's okay," Sky said. "The world will always be filled with amps. I can hear the word."

"Right, just sorry, sorry!" Joe said.

"We're all sorry," Chris Wiley said. "We'll miss your dad 'til the day we die ourselves, Sky. He wasn't just a bandmate and a friend, he was one of the finest men I've ever known."

"Thank you. And it's okay. Seriously," Sky said. She looked around.

And she thought of the years and years her dad had played with Skyhawk. Like Chris had said, these guys weren't just workmates, they had been Jake's friends, dear friends, more family than anything else.

How could she possibly believe one of them may have wanted him dead?

"Okay, I have date night with the old ball and chain," Mark said. "Ouch! Did I say that? I meant my beloved wife. Hmm. No wonder your dad wrote the best ballads, Sky. I'm a jerk. I love Susie, been with her thirty years, so…"

Sky laughed. "It's okay. You can joke around me, too."

"Yeah, just offensive, but cool," Joe assured him. "Anyway…"

Mark waved and headed toward the door. He paused, looking back. "Chris, Joe, Hank and I have been doing these songs forever, and you three—Brandon, Chase, Sky—have sat in at various times through the years. But I never expected today to go this well. Okay, so…for some of us, after all these years, it would be pathetic if we weren't in sync, but you kids were. Well, thanks, and great!"

"Thank you, Mark," Chase said. Sky smiled and nodded, ready to head out herself. This rehearsal had been her return intro.

Now she needed to think. Maybe make a few notes.

A few notes about what? Did she think if one of them was guilty, they would just fall apart in front of her today?

"I'm heading out for a beer after that," Brandon said. "Anyone want to join me?"

"I'll go with you, kid," his father said. "Joe?"

"Yeah, sure. I'm in," Joe said.

"Sky, come on!" Brandon said.

"Maybe tomorrow night. I didn't sleep well. A little nervous, maybe," she lied.

"We'll hold you to it!" Chris said.

"Chase?" Brandon asked. "You're not going to make me go out alone with the old guys, are you?"

"Rain check for tomorrow night, too," Chase said. "I have some work—"

"Work! Why do you work when you could hit the road with us forever?" Mark asked him. "Your granddad would love it!"

"I love sitting in. Not sure I'm ready to be a forever drummer," Chase said. "Anyway, good night, all!"

He headed out as well with everyone trailing him. They waved again, breaking apart to head to their various parking places.

Sky was in a garage off Canal, and she walked down the street, deep in thought at first.

Then something seemed to disturb her; she *felt* as if she was being followed.

When she stopped and turned to search the area, no one was there. Well, people were there, but no one who seemed to be paying the least bit of attention to her.

No one from Skyhawk.

She shook her head, wondering again if she wasn't crazy and if she wasn't letting her suspicion turn to paranoia.

With a shake of her head, she hurried on to the garage.

It wasn't until she reached her car on the third level that she stopped dead, staring.

Chase was there. Leaning against the front of her little SUV, arms crossed casually over his chest as he watched her approach.

"What are you doing here?" she demanded.

But he shook his head, staring at her curiously. "The question is this. What the hell do you think you're doing?"

She angled her head and narrowed her eyes. "I'm taking my dad's place. Just like you're sitting in for Hank—"

"I've sat in before. You've avoided the band like the plague."

"I've changed my mind."

He walked over to her, not touching her, just standing a few inches from her. "I know you," he said softly. "And I know how you felt about your father. I don't know what you're up to, but I do know this. You've got to be careful, Sky."

"I'm not up to anything. Why should I be careful? My dad died because of a tragic accident, right?"

"Please, be careful."

He turned and left her. She saw that he had parked in the same area of the garage.

Had he followed her?

He was already in his car.

"Chase!" she called, walking toward him. His engine was running.

She stepped in front of his car. He wasn't going to hit her; she was sure of that.

Of course, he didn't. He looked to the side.

She walked around to the driver's seat. He lowered his window.

"Why do I need to be careful? What do you know? Who do you think—"

"I don't know anything, Sky. But if there was anything to know, you slinking about trying to make someone guilty of something could put you in extreme danger."

"You do know something," she said.

He let out a soft sigh, staring straight ahead. "Again, I don't *know* anything. But I do know if there's anything to know, you snooping around could put you in danger. Sky, just—"

"You're just repeating yourself. I don't need you to worry about me," she said.

He turned and studied her. "Yeah. You made that perfectly clear a few years back," he said softly. "But you know, sorry, in memory of your father, I worry about you anyway."

She was suddenly afraid she might burst into tears. And it was all so ridiculous. She had walked away. Her father's death had been devastating to her, and she'd probably hurt herself—and her mother—with the way she'd retreated inward.

But that was long ago now. And she'd heard that Chase had moved on. He had kept studying, but he'd sat in with other groups in the past years. He'd been seen with a few of the hottest, newest female acts out there.

She lowered her head. She wasn't about to cry.

"My father didn't make a mistake with an amp," she

said simply. "Sorry. Something happened the night he died. And since you're so determined that I'm up to something, you might as well know I will never accept that it was his fault in any way. Good night."

She turned to head back to her own car.

And she wasn't sure if she was relieved or disappointed that he didn't follow her.

If she closed her eyes, she could remember the past too clearly.

Along with all she had so foolishly thrown away.

Chapter Two

"Well?"

"Well?" Chase replied.

He'd come home to find his supervising director, Andy Wellington, was on his couch, stretched back comfortably, watching a sitcom and waiting for him.

Of course, Wellington had necessarily approved his undercover investigation into the death of Jake Ferguson. That he had done so had surprised Chase—Jake's death had been accepted as an accident and had occurred years earlier. Even if it had been deemed suspicious in any way, a homicide case would have been tossed in with the rest of the cold cases by now.

Wellington didn't have a personal interest in the case; he'd admired Jake Ferguson and liked the fact his undercover agent was part of the music world.

But his interest wasn't personal, and customarily, Chase's personal interest would have kept him on the sidelines.

But it was hard to find his kind of an in.

Chase had meant to take part in the show, one way or the other. But he'd expected he'd be taking personal days to do it, and Wellington might have even tried to stop him for being too close to any possible suspects if there was a case. Then, of course, he would have had to try to convince Wellington that no, he was just sitting in for his grandfather and if he didn't, it could injure any good Chase did in undercover work since it was known—by hardened fans, at least—that he was the grandson of legendary rock drummer Hank McCoy.

Wellington sat up, folding his hands idly on his knees as he waited for Chase to talk.

The man was a good boss. Chase had read up on him and knew he was fifty-one, married, with two kids in college. He'd started in the field just like the agents he supervised now and worked his way up to his position, one he'd held for almost ten years. He could have a stern demeanor or a casual one. Six one, with a clean-cut head of silver hair and dark brown eyes, he was an impressive figure who could also look like a friendly dad.

"So? Anything?"

"Yeah, a good session," Chase told him. He shook his head. "I have known these guys my whole life—Joe Garcia, Mark Reynolds, Chris Wiley and, of course, my grandfather, Brandon, Chris's son and Skylar Ferguson. We rented the space—no roadies were with us."

"And you want to believe it was a roadie and not a friend you've known all your life," Wellington said flatly. He lifted his hands in the air. "That's all well and good, except this person has to be someone who had worked with the group time and again. The particular—and deadly—brand of stuff they discovered has shown up in every area where the band played."

"Yes, I want to believe a roadie is involved. And that it's not Joe, Mark or Chris. Honestly, I think I'd know if it was my grandfather, and you know that—"

"Yes, he's rehabbing from heart surgery," Wellington said.

"And," Chase told him, "a roadie would have had greater access to the stage and the stage equipment—including the amps."

"There is logic in that. Just don't wear blinders."

"I never wear blinders."

"But what you think is that Jake Ferguson was killed because he suspected what was going on, that someone involved was selling drugs, and he had to be shut up before he turned them in?"

Chase hesitated and shrugged. "Yeah," he said at last. "And, yes, it shouldn't be, but it is personal in a way. Jake was clean as a whistle. He had been since he'd returned from fighting in Vietnam. He wasn't a monster who lit on anyone who ordered a beer, and if his friends wanted to light up a joint here or there, he could shrug it off. But he would have never tolerated someone selling drugs—especially when so many customers might be kids or young adults. And especially since the drugs had been showing up now and then where their shows had been playing. Yes, Jake was killed, I'm convinced, and for a reason. The same reason that has you agreeing with me, when protocol suggests that it's not."

Wellington actually grinned. "Yeah. I can't bring back your rock-star friend. If my sanctioning your investigation while 'just playing with your gramps's band' can manage that, then I can blink easily enough. But you will keep me posted every step of the way."

Chase nodded. For a minute, he wondered if he should tell Wellington he was worried. Skylar Ferguson didn't know a thing about the suspicions the FBI was harboring regarding drug sales revolving around the band, but she didn't believe her father's death had been an accident.

It worried him. It might worry Wellington enough to pull the plug.

Then he'd be more worried than ever about Sky, Chase knew.

And, really, what could he say about Skylar?

"So, is it going to be a hell of a show? Shake the arena?" Wellington asked.

"You bet."

"And you have tickets for me, right?"

"Backstage passes included, Uncle Andy," Chase assured him.

Wellington frowned at that.

"It's cool," Chase assured him. "We all called friends Aunt this or Uncle that back when I was growing up. They'll just think you're a family friend they've never met."

"But your folks—"

"Aren't coming. They've been in Ireland for the last six months. My dad flew in and out to make sure I was taking good care of *his* father. This has been a great opportunity for my mom, working at the museum in Dublin, so Gramps and I both insisted that Dad get back over there."

Wellington nodded. "I trust you. Obviously, you wouldn't be working for me if I didn't. All right, so I'm out of here for tonight."

Chase stood to walk him out.

"Great place you have here," Wellington told him, standing on the porch and looking toward the path that led around to the side courtyard. "You're right in the French Quarter, away from the fury of Bourbon Street, just two blocks off Esplanade and about that distance in from Rampart. Very oddly neighborhood-y."

Chase grinned. "Yeah. My grandfather, Hank, bought

this place when the city was a disaster, right after Katrina. He paid too much for it, but he's a good guy, too. The family he bought it from was in trouble, no jobs, kids in college… And, yeah, I have to admit, being the grandson of a rock icon has its perks. He gave me the house as a gift when I graduated from college."

"You grew up here."

"Yeah, in New Orleans. In a house my folks still own in the Irish Channel area."

"And you're working for me," Wellington said, shaking his head.

"They still call it home, but they travel all the time."

Wellington looked around, nodding. "Well, keep your head down. See you rockin' out."

Chase nodded and watched Wellington walk away, headed down the street. He paused for a minute. No way out of it, his grandfather's success—or the success of Skyhawk—had given him amazing privileges. But he had always known that, and he had known it was because his grandfather, like Jake Ferguson, was just a good guy. From the time he'd been a child he'd been taught they were blessed and lucky and that meant they had to help others. Hank McCoy had practiced what he preached, and he was one of the few people who knew what Chase really did and who he worked for. Hank had been surprised at first about Chase's deepening interest in criminology. But when Chase had been about to graduate with his second degree, he'd told Hank a little impatiently, "You told me to help people, that we'd led a charmed life and that meant giving back. Gramps, I think I can be good at delving into things, discovering the truth. I think I can really help people this way!"

Hank had grown silent, and then he'd smiled.

"All right. Maybe you're right. But don't forget the drums, huh?"

"I love the drums. And the guitar, though I'm better at drums."

"Genetics," Hank told him. "Go out and save the world. Do me proud. But remember this. Music. Seriously. Like love, it makes the world go around."

Chase headed back in, locked the door, grimacing when he remembered it had been his idea to give Wellington a key for the times now when he might be waiting to see him privately, wanting a personal update.

His office was on the right side of the house, just behind the music room. He headed there, determined to go over everything he knew about the major players in the case.

Of course, that started with the band.

And his memories of the last concert Jake had played, and the last words Jake had said to him.

There had been about seventy thousand people in the audience, just as there had been for U2 and the Rolling Stones.

Seventy thousand suspects?

No. Because Jake wouldn't have known or had contact with the majority of the audience, though of course, New Orleans had been his hometown, so he'd have had friends there. And the other band members would have had friends. And family.

But Jake wouldn't have been talking with many people right before the show: he'd have been with the band, with the roadies and perhaps the venue supervisor. But he was angry about something he'd seen just as they had been setting up. Something he had seen someone do.

And because of the emotion involved, it suggested someone close to him.

Back to the band and the roadies.

Sometimes, roadies were attached to a venue, sometimes to a performer or group, and sometimes, a combination of the two were working.

That night…

Chase closed his eyes and leaned back. Though he'd already been intrigued by other courses in college, his focus in life that night had been music. And he'd been standing stage left, ready to sit in for Hank, something that still thrilled his grandfather since his father had chosen to follow another path, the restoration of ancient art pieces. Chase's father's work was impressive since he'd worked on pieces in major museums across the world—it just didn't compare to the fame of being a rock star. Though Chase had failed miserably at drawing so much as a stick figure, his dad had never minded that he didn't follow him into the art world, but rather he was glad that Chase made Hank so happy.

Jake hadn't just been the lead singer. He'd been the true front man. He knew how to work a crowd. He also knew how to share, kicking over to other band members, never doing a show that didn't feature each player, each instrument.

After his death…

The gigs hadn't been enormous. Joe Garcia had taken over most of the vocals, Hank had taken on a few, and Chris and Mark the rest. During his life, Jake Ferguson had recorded sessions with his daughter, wildly popular on social media through the years.

Everyone had been beyond thrilled that she had agreed

to be part of this concert. It was taking place in her hometown, and the guys had assumed that she had finally agreed in a moment of weakness. She'd never shown any of them hostility; she had always been not just cordial but friendly because she didn't ever want to ruin the fact that her mom was still friends with the group and their families and when she'd been at the same place at the same time, she'd hung out with them.

But Chase knew her better. Even if it had been years now since…

They'd been together.

He winced. They'd been darlings on stage together, beloved by the group and by the crowds. So young and sweet in their puppy love, and how perfect that the grandson of the drummer and the daughter of the vocalist and lead guitarist should fall in love.

It wasn't their time together on stage that he remembered.

It was her laughter, her smile, her eyes when she looked at him. Her way of making sure that she tipped any musician they ever saw playing on the street—and there were plenty. It was the spring break when they'd escaped their families and everyone to head to St. Augustine Beach. Days in the sun, nights spent on history and ghost tours and just being together.

And then Jake had died. And she'd never said another word to him; she'd stepped away. And when he'd tried to reach her after the funeral, she had told him that she couldn't, just couldn't, see him again. Ever.

After today, he thought, leaning back and stretching in his desk chair, he knew why.

To the best of his knowledge, she'd never taken any

courses in criminology. And she hadn't been near the stage when her father had died.

She couldn't have heard her father's last words—spoken just to Chase as he'd taken over for Hank on a number—so she couldn't have his reasons for suspecting that something more than an accident had been involved.

But she thought that someone in the band had killed her father. And she had surely had him on that list along with Hank.

He was convinced himself that whoever Jake had been talking about had realized that Jake was going to blow the whistle on them.

Who it was and what they had done, Chase didn't know for sure. But he suspected that it was selling drugs, that they were responsible for the contaminated drugs that had killed several people, young people among them, in the areas where the band had played.

Jake's last words had echoed in his head through the years.

"I know what's going on, and I saw... I'm going to put an end to it as soon as this gig is over!"

Then his showman's smile had taken over his face, and he'd stepped into the spotlight.

He'd seen something. Someone. And he'd meant to call the cops when the lights were down and the music and applause and screams in the crowds had ended. Whoever had been selling drugs would have known that if Jake had seen them, it was all over. He'd cleaned up the hard way himself; he'd seen too many people die who had lost their grip.

And he had known whatever he knew before the show started...

Chris Wiley, Joe Garcia, Mark Reynolds, and, of course, Chase's own grandfather, Hank McCoy.

He knew his grandfather didn't do drugs. No one could hide drug use that well, especially on the rock trail. In his time getting to meet or know about some of the most famous musicians out there, he'd seen too many who had been lost to addictions. He'd also seen those who had started out with some hard partying—something easy to fall into when you were young and suddenly rich and famous—but totally cleaned up their acts and were still performing at the ages when many people were ready to hang up their hats.

But Skyhawk…

He shook his head. Joe Garcia had never done drugs, but he still enjoyed a few beers. Mark Reynolds was known to chill with a little marijuana.

To his knowledge, none of them did cocaine, heroin or any of the hard stuff. Then again, the best dealers probably never touched the stuff themselves.

They were the four surviving original members of Skyhawk. He sat in sometimes, Sky had come with her dad, and Brandon Wiley sat in for Chris.

Sometimes, Sky's mom had come up as well.

Joe Garcia was married. Mark's one son was the CEO of a major tech company, one he had created himself. His name was David. He always seemed to be a great guy, proud of his dad who was, in turn, proud of him. Mark had shrugged when people had asked him if he hadn't wanted his only child following in his footsteps. "Just glad I could pay for the education that helped him get where he is today!" Mark said.

Then, of course, there were the roadies. The band had

three that were on their payroll. Justin West, Charlie Bentley and Nathan Harrison. They were in their forties, men who had started with Skywalk at least twenty years ago when they'd been in their twenties themselves, young and eager to be with such a prestigious band.

So…

That was his suspect pool. Four surviving band members—their family members at the stage that night—himself, Sky and Brandon—and the roadies.

He was forgetting one person. Kenneth Malcolm.

Malcolm. Malcolm worked the venue. But…

The effects of the strange drug sales that seemed to follow Skyhawk had been found in various places, not just New Orleans. So that should eliminate Malcolm, but…

Sky.

He bit his lower lip, shaking his head.

She had been so loyal to her father, and he understood why. Jake had been amazing; he'd been amazing to Chase as well, all of his life. A man who truly believed in the human family and in his responsibility to give when giving was needed. The band had begun in a garage in New Orleans, but Jake had been there not just for the aftermath of Katrina, but for any other disaster hitting the country as well. He encouraged the young. He was dedicated to education for everyone. He could joke and laugh and somehow be a kind human being with the strength of steel.

That show…

He could close his eyes and still see the massive concert. The seats and floor filled, people watching and waiting, the light show beginning, the display of the colors over the crowd, over the stage, blues, pinks, reds, more.

The venue host welcoming "the amazing Skyhawk"

to the stage, the band members heading out and Jake at the mic, welcoming and thanking the crowd, the beat of the drums, the chords of the guitar as Jake strummed the first notes, and the bass and rhythm and the keyboards coming in…

The crowd screaming as they began, the vibrancy, the excitement in the arena…

The first hour had gone brilliantly. Jake had called out for Hank's drum solo, he had highlighted Chris on bass, Joe on the keyboards, and Mark on the rhythm guitar. All the solos had ended with the group coming in together again, setting off into a medley of several songs. Then Jake had announced that a family member was stepping in, and Chase would be drumming. He'd walked off to escort Chase to the drums as Hank had bowed and taken off to the side. Chase had heard Jake muttering those last words, then Mark had warned there was something wrong with the amp and then…

Jake had exclaimed to the audience, "Give me a sec here, my friends… Don't want anything missed for my hometown crowd!"

They had applauded and screeched out their appreciation, and Jake had walked over to the amp and there had been a spark, a small spark, and then a sizzle that had seemed to burst through the entire massive arena before the explosion at the amp, the burst of flames…

Smoke and screams. Security trying to initiate evacuation, roadies trying to reach the band, and Jake…

Jake lying there, eyes wide open, even in death, his look stunned as the fire burned around him, charred his body…

He'd tried to run to Jake. Someone had caught him, screaming he'd been burned alive, and dragged him back to the wings and offstage and out into the night air while he'd screamed and screamed himself, knowing that Sky was there, that she would run right into the blaze.

He understood Sky's feelings, but still…

He stood suddenly. He had to talk to her. She really didn't understand what she could be setting herself up for.

He headed to the front door.

The years had been so strange. They'd avoided each other in an area that was close. Then again, he'd been studying and then working, and his strange job had taken him around the country just as it had now taken him home.

His hometown. Yes, it was where Skyhawk had begun, where Jake had lived next door to Chris Wiley, and the others had been nearby. Jake had been writing lyrics for years, strumming notes to them, and with the others, the music had been created to go with the words, and bit by bit, they had formed their first album, scraped together the money for the studio to get it recorded…

And history had been made.

It was where Jake had been born, and where he had died.

And where Chase was suddenly extremely worried that Sky Ferguson, named for the band itself, might well die.

He couldn't let it happen.

She was so determined. But she didn't know what she was doing.

She didn't know the suspected why of his death, why a killer would seek a way to end his life before Jake's sense of life and justice might bring down that quiet and subtle killer…

Yes. Time to pay her a visit.

SKY WAS STARING blankly at her schedule for the coming week. She had determined that she was going to keep moving when she wasn't with the band, but despite her resolve and opening the computer, she was simply staring at the screen, moments of the past seizing what was supposed to be her focus on the present.

She hadn't scheduled work for the next few weeks, determined that she would do the show and work with whatever aftermath there might be. She had never left music behind but rather turned it into something that gave her real pleasure. She took music lessons to troubled kids, kids of any age. Sometimes, it was working with four- and five-year-olds with behavioral issues as they entered prekindergarten. Sometimes, it was working with teens who were acting out. She'd become a certified therapist with her specialty, but she'd also discovered that the theater classes she'd taken worked well with it all, especially those in improv. Other times, she worked one-on-one with children or sat in on classes. She used her mother's maiden name as her business name, and while students often knew who she was, they thought it fun to keep the secret. The little kids had no clue what *Skyhawk* was anyway, but for the teens, it was a nice thrill that made them respect her with a bit more awe.

She traveled wherever she was needed. She had discovered that doing what she did was great for the mind. Keeping at what she did, of course, she'd never get rich. But she didn't need to get rich. Her dad had seen to it that she and her mom were taken care of for life.

She closed her eyes for a minute, wincing. She was glad to be home. She had a wonderful old house in the Garden District, secluded behind a tall stonework wall and gate.

The home was one of the oldest in the district, and when they'd bought the place, they'd had to redo all the plumbing and electric, the kitchen and the bathrooms. But she had worked on the house with her dad who had never minded getting his hands dirty. He never expected others to accomplish every piece of what he saw as his manual labor. And, she remembered, smiling, he had also told her that they never knew when the tide might change, when his music might become something that was seldom played and of the past. The world could be a fickle place.

She started when she heard the buzzer that meant someone was at her gate. She hadn't been expecting any friends that night: they all knew that she was going to perform with Skyhawk.

But there was a telecom on her desk, and she pushed the button. "Hello?"

"It's me, Skylar. Let me in, please."

Her heart seemed to skip a beat. Seeing Chase again…

She had been so head over heels in love with him. And then she had just walked away. He'd tried to reach her.

But…

It had seemed the only way to get through her father's death had been to turn away from Skyhawk and anything and everything that had to do with it. That included the people.

And so—as she had found herself prone to do several times during her life—she had cut off her nose to spite her face.

Now, seeing him again… Nothing had changed about him that would alter her concept of what she had seen in him years ago. He was still a striking individual. No matter the passage of time, she still felt as if she…as if she could just touch him. Crawl into his arms, maybe now, at last, feel something in his warmth that was comforting to the soul…

And probably so much more! she told herself dryly.

"Skylar? I need to speak with you," he said impatiently.

Of course, he was impatient. She had been the one to build the wall. And whatever it was that he wanted…

Well, maybe his empathy had come to an end.

"Sorry. I'm here." She still hesitated, wincing. Then she pushed the button that would open the gate and then the front door.

She pushed away from her desk and hurried out to greet him at the entry.

He opened the door and stepped in. "Hey, um, sorry," she murmured.

He arched a brow to her. "For answering the door slowly? Or being incredibly rude for year upon year?"

She made a face at him.

"Sorry," he said with a shrug. "That's not why I'm here."

"Why are you here?"

"You. I'm worried about you," he told her.

She frowned. "Why?"

"Because, whether you like to admit it or not, I know you. You loved Skyhawk when your dad was alive. Now you hate it and everyone and everything around it."

"*Hate* is a strong word."

"So what are you doing?"

She shrugged, trying to avoid his eyes. He had always seen too much. He did now with her. More than physical attraction, it was part of what had made them such an incredible couple: they knew one another. They understood their different family dynamics. They'd respected one another's thoughts, shared explanations…

"Kind of late, but would you like some coffee? Soda, water? I may have something stronger, a beer maybe?" she suggested.

"Let's have coffee," he suggested.

"Uh…okay."

He led the way to the kitchen. Apparently, she hadn't changed much of anything through the years. She had a new coffee maker with all the bells and whistles for just about any kind of coffee someone might like, but it sat right where the old one had with the pods in a little drawer attached to the machine.

"Regular with a hint of cream?" he asked her.

"Yeah. Black?" she asked in turn.

"Yeah. I guess coffee tastes don't change through the years."

"Oh, but they do!" she protested. "I sometimes enjoy an espresso, straight and strong, and on occasion a vanilla latte."

He didn't respond.

"And you?"

"Espresso, black."

"Well, it's something," she murmured.

She headed to the refrigerator, getting cream for her coffee. He'd made hers first, so she added cream to her cup while he put through a second.

"Got any food?" he asked her.

"I'm not sure I invited you to dinner…"

"Dinner was hours ago. It's going on breakfast. I'll settle for—"

"You always were hungry. You must have the metabolism of a hummingbird."

"That doesn't answer the question."

She sighed. "What do you want? Yes, I keep food here. I know... I have cheese grits and shrimp in the fridge from yesterday, should still be good."

"Perfect."

"I'll just microwave a dish—"

"No, I'll heat them up on the stove," he said casually. "Hey, Hank always hated the microwave—said it was giving us weird brain waves. I'm not antimicrowave, just learned that a lot of things heat up better on a stove."

"Knock yourself out," Sky said. She opened the refrigerator again, digging out the container with her leftovers. She handed it to him. "There's quite a lot there. I placed an order and didn't realize I'd ordered the family size until I got home. They didn't have that kind of ordering before the pandemic years, but during that time, I guess they learned that people decided they liked picking things up to take home."

He knew to look in the lower cabinet next to the stove for the frying pan.

Sky thought that she really needed to change up her life a bit.

"Where's your mom, by the way?" Chase asked her. "Is she coming to the concert?"

"She wasn't planning to. She's in Ireland with her sister. They're doing a whole heritage kind of a thing. But..."

"Now that she knows you're going to be taking on your dad's role, she wants to come?"

Sky sighed. "Yep. I told her she's heard me all her life. That she knew Skyhawk all her life. She doesn't need to come."

"Did you argue her out of it?"

Sky shrugged. “I hope!”

“Ah, which leads to a further question.”

“I didn’t think you came just for shrimp and grits.”

“Cheaper than a restaurant,” he said.

“Right. Like you need to worry about that. Just what are you doing now? Working in some kind of lab somewhere? Never seemed like you.”

“Call me a perpetual student,” he said lightly, using a spatula to move the grits around in the pan as they heated. “Anyway, if it was just to see you sing your dad’s songs, why wouldn’t you want your mom here?”

“It’s not a matter of not wanting her,” Sky said. “I just don’t want her feeling that she has to leave a trip she’s wanted to do to come back for what she’s already done.”

“You’re lying, aren’t you?” he asked her.

“Why would I be lying?”

“Because you don’t want me to know the truth,” he said quietly.

Again, she felt as if her heart skipped a beat, froze in her chest.

He did know her too well.

“I don’t know what you’re talking about,” Sky lied.

He turned off the stove and lifted the frying pan, setting it on a cold burner. He turned to her, his hands on his hips, and she knew why he had come.

Of course.

“Sky,” he said flatly, “you think that someone deliberately killed your father. And you think that somehow, doing this show, you’re going to figure out how and why. But that’s crazy. Don’t you see that it’s crazy? It’s been years now. Even if we were all forensic scientists, it would be too late. No clues would have survived this amount of time, this amount of people in and out—"

She didn't realize that she'd walked over to him until she set her hand on his arm, shaking her head in protest and interrupting. "You've taken too many classes! It's just New Orleans. Hometown. I said that I'd do my dad's songs, that I'd be him for this."

He looked at her a long moment. She realized she had come too close. She still remembered far too much about him, the scent of him, the feel of him, and in that moment, she wanted to forget all her misery, to lay her head against his shoulder and let him hold her and tell her that everything would be all right and then…

And then touch her and let the touch become something deeper and more intimate and then, in his very special way, make her forget for a while that anything in the universe could be wrong, that there was light and beauty and incredible wonder in the place that he could take her to…a place that they never really left because they remained curled together, legs draped over legs, flesh still damp and hot and touching…

"Sorry!" she murmured. "I just—"

"You never need to be sorry with me," he said softly.

She had to step farther back, make a much lighter situation out of it.

"Oh, thought you came here tonight so that I could give you a massive apology!" she teased.

He smiled. "Oh, trust me, I haven't expected that for years." His expression grew serious again. "I meant that you never needed to apologize for touching me."

"Your grits!"

He turned to look at the pan. "Yeah. They're still there."

"Getting cold. I'll get you a dish," she said.

"Get yourself one, too."

"I'm not hungry—"

"You're never hungry until I'm eating and then you're hungry. Get two dishes."

She hadn't realized it, but he'd made her smile again.

She got two plates.

He spooned the shrimp and cheese grits onto both of them, and they sat at the kitchen table.

"I wasn't expecting dinner—"

"I already tried to tell you," Sky said. "Dinner was hours ago."

"I wasn't planning on a meal—"

"You asked for one."

"You might have refused. So this is nice. And still…"

"You came to warn me that I shouldn't mess with the past, that doing so would be worthless," Sky said. "I'm just singing."

"Stop lying."

"Just singing and playing the guitar."

"Sky." He looked at her while chewing and swallowing. He set his fork down and took a sip of his coffee.

She realized she had frozen, watching him.

He reached over and took her hand.

"You know, I love you. From the minute I first saw you, I think even as kids, I was in awe of you and in love with you. But that's really neither here nor there as far as this all goes. Sky. Listen to me. Leave it alone. Sing, play, have a good time, honor your father. He wrote great songs. He reigned with the hottest band over several decades. But don't do anything else. Don't question people. Don't interrogate the roadies. Leave it."

"Why? If everything was so innocent—"

She was startled when he winced and slammed a fist on the table.

"Sky! Listen to me, damn it! Don't you understand? If any of this was real, anything you suspect at all, then you'd be putting yourself in danger. Honor your father, Sky! How the hell do you think Jake would feel if you died because of him?"

Chapter Three

Chase had tried. He had tried everything in hell and in his legal power.

He couldn't just knock her out, kidnap her and keep her away until after the show.

Well, he could. But it wouldn't be legal. And that would definitely be something that she wouldn't forgive.

"Chase," Sky said, looking steadily at him, "trust me. I have no intention of getting myself killed. And the fact that you're here tells me something."

"That I'm a glutton for punishment?" he said dryly.

She let out a sound of exasperation. "No! You think that something is off-kilter, too. You know that what happened to my father was not an accident. You don't know what happened, but you know that something was wrong. Very wrong."

"Sky—"

"What? It's okay for you to be there and suspicious as all hell but not me?"

"Sky, first—"

"There is no *first*."

"Well, yeah, there is," he told her. "You know what I've been doing. I got my major in criminology and I've kept at it—"

"Professional student, yeah, I got it."

"No, you don't. Yes, I've taken a lot of classes about poisons, blood spatter, DNA and fingerprints. But I've also spent hours upon hours at a shooting range. I know how to use a gun. I know how to aim. I've taken classes in self-defense—"

"And would a gun have protected my father from an amp that had been purposely set up with a frayed wire, something timed to go off after the show started? Was he going to shoot at the electricity?" Sky demanded.

"Okay, no," Chase agreed. She had a point.

"I'll be on stage, you'll be on stage," she reminded him passionately.

He sighed, looking down, shaking his head.

"Look at me, Chase, please!" Sky begged. "I know you, too, remember? I know that you suspect that someone on the stage that night—or near it, someone with easy access to the instruments and the amps—meant for my father to die. I can't begin to understand why anyone would want to kill him. Everyone loved him—seriously. He—"

"Sky, stop. Yeah, he was one of the nicest human beings I have ever encountered. One of the best. But he was no doormat. He held his own when he had an opinion. And he was always a staunch defender of anyone he saw as downtrodden."

"So," she said slowly, studying him, "you do know that he was killed."

"Sky, I don't *know*—"

"You suspect. And you've figured out what I hadn't—that he was probably killed because he was going to do something for someone and someone else didn't want him doing it, or—"

"Sky, don't you understand? That's why it's dangerous."

She nodded. "I repeat. I'll be on stage. You'll be on stage."

"I'm not going to talk you out of this," Chase said.

She shook her head.

"All right. Then, do me a favor," he said.

"Of course."

"You let me know anything that you think, feel or suspect," he told her.

"On one condition."

"What's that?"

"You let me know anything that *you* think, feel or suspect," she said sweetly.

He let out a sound of aggravation.

"That's the deal," she told him.

"All right, then, I have another idea," he said.

"Let's hear it."

"Okay, we're in this together, that's what you want?"

"*Demand* is more like it," she said casually.

"Then, we pretend that we're a thing again. That way, I can be at your side. That way, I can at least attempt to protect you."

She looked startled for a minute, and then as if she was about to protest.

But she didn't. Instead, she smiled. "At least that way, maybe *I* can protect *you*."

"Sure, cute, of course," he said. "The point is we stick together and we have one another's backs. How does that work for you?"

She nodded slowly. "There's not a lot of time. I've made lists of everyone there—"

"I did, too."

"But," Sky continued, frustrated then, "we only have two more rehearsals and then the show."

"Lunch."

Sky's face knotted in confusion. "Lunch? It's past midnight, and you've just finished a nice big plate of cheese grits and shrimp and—"

"No. Let's invite the guys to lunch."

"Oh! Smart. Think they'll come?"

"To the best of my knowledge, they have nothing else to do until the show. Brandon Wiley is the only other family member, and he's here with Chris, so they'd be having lunch together somewhere anyway. Of course, every one of the guys—"

"We need the roadies, too," she reminded him.

"They'll come. It will be a free meal."

"Okay, so..."

"Why don't we send out an email invitation," Chase said.

"We?"

He smiled. "Of course. We're a thing, right?"

"I'll write it or you'll write it?" Sky asked.

"Doesn't matter, we just need to get it out."

Sky nodded, rose and walked from the kitchen to the dining room and back across to her office. She sat at her computer and started filling in addresses. "Okay, I have Chris, Mark, Hank, Joe and Brandon. Not sure I have all the roadies in my address book."

"I'll fill them in," Chase said. "May I?"

She shrugged and started out of her chair. He was already sliding in before she could slide out. She moved quickly.

Chase entered the extra addresses and then a message.

Hey, guys! Rare opportunity! Lunch in the French Quarter—seriously! We'll meet at Chase's noonish, unless that's too early for old rock stars.

"Your place?" Sky asked. "I thought you meant here."

"My place is more convenient for those not living here—French Quarter."

"Okay, whatever. But as for lunch…"

"Delivery. It will be great."

Sky looked at him, nodding. A little blip caused them both to look at the computer screen. "An answer already," Chase noted.

Sky stood to look over his shoulder. "Joe Garcia! He says he's in. Excellent. And he gave us an LOL, telling us that old people have a tendency to be early risers!"

"We'll have them all here, trust me," Chase said. "And—"

He broke off. A dog was barking loudly enough to raise the dead. The sound was coming from somewhere nearby.

From right next door.

Chase leaped to his feet and hurried out of Skylar's office to the front, throwing open the door.

He could swear he saw the gate at the front rattling. And the dog continued to bark. He hurried outside, looking just beyond the gate.

There was nothing. And the barking stopped abruptly.

"Chase!" Sky called, hurrying outside to join him. "Hey, people walk on the street. And that's King from next door, a big old shepherd, but sweet as a baby. He's—"

"He's what you need," Chase told her.

"Chase—"

"Let's get back in. You need a big old dog like King."

"I love dogs. But I travel too much. And, please, come

on, Chase, this is getting ridiculous! No one is going to come after me here. I mean, why would they? As far as anyone knows, I'm filling in for my dad. It's just a show, a show—"

"Unlike any other," he said. "Damn, Sky, if I know what you're up to, someone else may suspect that you're looking for them, too. Move."

"Right. And not you?"

"Jake wasn't my dad," he said quietly. "I loved him, but others loved him, too. Come on. Let's get back in the house."

"But seriously, I have the gate, you have to buzz to get in—"

"Or jump the wall."

"King is out there," Sky reminded him.

"All night?" he demanded. She wasn't going to lie. She shook her head.

"But still—"

"I'm not leaving."

"What?"

"I'm not leaving."

"I'm not inviting you to stay!"

"You don't even have your own dog."

"I'll get one tomorrow," Sky promised.

King suddenly started barking again. Chase couldn't leave her. Whether she liked it or not, he couldn't leave her. And it would be hell all night, knowing that she was upstairs, that they were close, that years had dripped away as if they'd never been apart, and he couldn't leave her.

"You have a lovely sofa," he said.

"That's not… I mean, the house has four bedrooms upstairs. Chase, you know that's not the point."

"Hey, we'll put on a good show."

What the hell did he have to do? Tell her the truth about what he now did for a living, the truth about who he worked for…

"Sky, I am worried for your life. Because someone besides me suspects that you're not just singing with the band for old times' sake, for your dad."

King barked and stopped again.

"I would appreciate a pillow and a blanket," he told her, prodding her through the entry to the parlor.

"Really? If you're insisting, there are guest rooms—"

"No, I'll be down here. Where I'll know if someone is fooling around with the house."

"Super hearing? After being a drummer?"

"Cushioning earplugs. Hank told me too many of his friends have gone deaf. You need someone else here. Sky, what the hell. This is real. Someone could break in. With a gun. You need protection. Tonight, I'm it."

"And what are you going to do if someone breaks in with a gun?" she asked.

"Shoot him," he said flatly.

CHASE WAS DOWNSTAIRS. Sky had provided him with two pillows and a blanket. The furniture in the large living area that consumed the center of the house was old—dating back to the 1800s—and she doubted that there was any way anyone could sleep comfortably on the one sofa that sat with a group of upholstered chairs in front of the fireplace.

But he was there.

Of course, she couldn't quite figure how she hadn't realized that he was armed. But she didn't know anything about guns. She'd never wanted to know anything about them, even when crime rates had gotten higher in many of the country's major cities.

And yet now…

She'd asked him, of course. With a shrug he'd explained it was all part of the classes he'd been taking in criminology, right along with blood spatter and fingerprints.

She'd provided him with the little he had asked for and he'd escaped.

But she knew he was there. And it was hell.

And then again, it wasn't.

While she was in a turmoil of hell where the past had come to life, she also felt…safe. She believed him. He knew how to use a firearm, and she figured he probably knew a lot more. He'd always been—perfect. Tall, broad-shouldered, lean-muscled, agile…a diver, a guy who could ski, skateboard, swim, kill it on a football field.

It had never occurred to her before to be afraid; she had simply been determined. In fact, even being her father's daughter, she'd never been afraid. The house was in a great quiet residential neighborhood, not too far from Lafayette Cemetery, Commander's Palace and a place she loved, Garden District Book Shop. Still close to a few iconic places, but private and off the beaten path. When she had turned eighteen, her parents had put the house in her name. When her dad had died, her mother had started traveling and when she was home, she liked to be in a little condo she'd purchased down in the French Quarter near Café du Monde.

Both of her parents had always been low-key, friends with their neighbors, quiet in their lifestyles when they weren't performing. They had loved being together. And yes, while he was recognizable, as he'd often explained with amusement, it just wasn't like being a movie star. The good majority of people in the world would have no idea of who he was when he walked down the street.

And she wasn't well known at all, so there had been no reason…

Of course, she could have done a few simple things. Like having alarms installed for the gate and the house. That might have meant that Chase McCoy wouldn't have insisted on spending a miserable night on her sofa.

And she wouldn't have spent the night knowing that he was there.

So much distance between them. Years! But…

When she was near him, all that they had shared might have been yesterday. She could remember the subtle way his scent, clean and masculine, could wrap around her: it was as if she could breathe him in. She loved the sound of his laughter, the look in his eyes…

And it was ridiculously tempting to walk down the stairs, just squeeze next to him, look up at him and pretend that time had not created a wall between them, a wall that she had somehow pushed into being.

But it was there. He was here because he was afraid for her. And because he had loved her father. And for no other reason.

She winced and tossed, plumping her pillow. She had to grow up. She couldn't erase the past, but it was behind her. She had to behave like a normal human being with him, except…

They were playing a game. A dangerous game. Pretending they were a couple who had simply fallen back together so that others might not suspect anything amiss if they whispered to one another, slipped together as a couple if they saw or heard something…

She had to grow up. Play the game. And for a minute, she was a little amused. Chase and all his criminology classes and work—doing whatever it was he did with most of his time.

Undercover!

Undercover in plain sight. And if it got her the answers she wanted, total justice for her father, well then, it was worth whatever she had to do.

Decided. Simple. Done.

And it was still the wee hours of the morning before exhaustion claimed her. Because he was there, downstairs, so close, and she didn't understand herself why she had thrown away such an incredible man, such a beautiful relationship.

SKY HAD STILL been sleeping when Chase called; he could hear it in her voice. He wondered if just maybe she'd had as much trouble falling asleep as he'd had. No matter. It was late. Time to move.

"Hello?" she murmured, curiosity in the very sleepiness of her voice.

"Time to rise and shine up in the… Sky!"

She groaned. "Oh, that was bad."

"Yeah, I know. But you need to wake up."

"Wait a minute. You're calling me—from downstairs?"

"Seemed the best way to wake you up," he told her.

"Okaaay."

"We need to get to my house."

"Um, the lunch thing, right. But it's still early."

"I know you want to shower. And then at my house, we'll

have to check our RSVPs and order the food in, I'll need to shower, and I'm hoping there's time for us to go through a few things."

"A few things?"

"Our suspect list, what we know about each of the players, the band, the roadies, anyone who might have been close. If what happened was more than an accident, there had to have been a reason."

She was quiet over the line for a minute. Then she told him, "You forgot something," she told him.

"What?"

"A dog? If I get a nice big dog, you get to go home at night."

He shook his head. "A nice big dog would be good, but I won't be leaving you."

She let out a sound of aggravation. "What? You're going to guard me the rest of my life?"

"I believe that between us, we'll glean the truth. We'll find out if there was more than the many law enforcement and fire personnel saw that day."

"They were looking for cause, not a reason," Sky murmured. "Should we make coffee first, grab something—"

"Believe it or not, I have coffee. And food. We need to go."

"I'm going to shower and come down," she said, ending the call.

CHASE LOOKED AT his phone for a minute, grimaced to himself and rose to wander the living room. The house was a beautiful one, but he knew that it had been falling apart when Jake had purchased it. He'd always loved period things.

There was a picture on the mantel, and he walked over to it. The photo had been taken when he and Sky had first started dating. But Hank was in it as well, along with Jake. It had been taken on stage one night, maybe at the casino stage in Florida, a smaller venue, maybe about seven thousand people, and it was one of the nights they had each come in for just a song or two. But the pride that both Jake and Hank wore on their faces was wide and touching, just like the way they all stood together, he and Sky in the middle, Hank and Jake flanking them.

He turned away from the picture, reminding himself that he was working. Someone in or connected to the band was selling drugs. Bad drugs. Not that they couldn't kill on their own, but these had been contaminated with fentanyl.

Jake had known it, and Jake had died.

And if there was anything he could do for Sky's father, it was going to be to keep his daughter safe. And between them, they would find the truth.

SKY HEADED FOR the shower. She realized she was arguing with him just to argue. She should be glad. Chase was on her side. Since she'd get nowhere by looking at the players and roadies and demanding to know if one of them had killed her father, it was great to have someone on her side.

Then again…

Hank McCoy was Chase's grandfather. And he was on the suspect list. Was Chase open to believing his own grandfather might have killed Jake?

She doubted it; if someone had told her that her father was a murderer, she wouldn't have believed it.

She turned the water on, not sure if she wanted it to

be hot and soothing or cold enough to really wake her up and straighten her out.

Sky tried both, and both were good. But she hurried and dressed quickly and casually in jeans and a tunic and hurried down the stairs.

"Let's go."

"Don't we both have cars here?" she asked.

"Leave yours."

"Why don't we leave yours?"

"Are you being argumentative for the sake of it? We're going to my house."

She winced. She was doing it again. Arguing just to argue.

"Fine. We'll take your car."

The distance between the Garden District and French Quarter wasn't great, but Jake was an expert of winding his way around the tourists who seemed to think it was fine to suddenly step out into the street at any given minute.

"The problem with the French Quarter," she murmured.

"Wandering tourists?" he asked. "No big deal. There's not so many this close to Esplanade and Rampart. Anyway…we made it."

He hit a button on a remote, and the gate that led to his courtyard swung open. He pulled his car into the garage, leaving room for those who were due to join them.

"They'll take rideshares or walk, depending on where they're staying," Sky commented.

"Probably, but just in case…we've some room here. And it's even possible to find spaces on this street this far from the river. Anyway, I've got to shower. I've ordered food, so if it gets here before I'm out—"

"I think it will be safe for me if I see that a food delivery is arriving."

He didn't reply but led the way through the kitchen entrance.

She remembered his home. And like her own, she thought, it was a great one. Having survived a number of serious fires, it was one of the oldest in the area, stemming from the late 1700s. But it had been treated with care through the years. It was a smaller house than hers with a narrower stairway, with touches of the period in the archways and architectural details. Her home was decidedly Victorian while his was more French Gothic, but both were part of what they loved about New Orleans: the history, the color and the music. Especially the music. She smiled, thinking about the wonderful performers she so often saw when she just took a walk down Royal Street.

"What?" Chase asked.

"What?"

"You're thinking something and smiling," Chase said.

"Just that I wonder… I mean, the guys started as kids, basically. My father being the grand old man in his twenties. And I wonder if they hadn't all grown up surrounded by so much great music if they would have become the group that they were. It wasn't one song—it wasn't a vocalist or a guitarist or any one instrument. These guys loved and grew up with and studied music, all of them," she said.

"As did we."

"And I still love it and use it, just in a different way," she assured him.

"Okay, so…the kitchen is smaller, but it has an island. So just in case—"

"I can safely handle food," she assured him.

"Okay, I'm headed upstairs."

"Go!"

He did, hurrying up the narrow flight that led to the second floor. He had a great balcony up there; they'd watched a few parades go by from that vantage point, though they took different routes now.

When he was gone, Sky slowly turned around, taking in the house. He'd either remained a fairly neat person or he had someone come in to clean. And while not the size of her place, he had a table in the dining area that stretched straight into the parlor that would seat eight, and there were plenty of sitting spaces in the parlor.

She walked to the left side of the house and found that one room was all but filled with a drum set. But Chase also played guitar, and he had a collection of tambourines and maracas. She smiled when she actually found a cowbell on the shelf along with the other smaller instruments.

What was he really doing with his life? she wondered.

When she'd hear about him through one of the band members or their families, he was just taking another class, sitting in with a group somewhere, working on something in a lab. He seemed to travel a lot, too.

She hadn't been there long before she heard a buzz and remembered that he had a gate bell, similar to the one she'd installed. She quickly headed for the front, freezing in the parlor when she looked up the stairs.

Chase was there, bottom half wrapped in a towel. His shoulders were bronzed and glistening, and his abs and pecs had remained smoothly muscled.

"I've got it!" she cried to him. "For God's sake, get dressed!"

"I don't know if you should answer the door—"

She ignored him, hurrying on to the front. She pushed the button at the door that opened the gate and stepped out to the porch. It was the food arriving, two burly men bearing boxes and bags. She greeted them pleasantly and directed them to the island in the kitchen and the long table in the dining room. They'd barely gotten things on the table when Chase came hurrying down, now in jeans, a T-shirt and a casual jacket.

She realized the latter probably concealed a weapon.

But he thanked the delivery men as well and saw them out.

"See?" she said. "Food, delivered, safely, and I managed it just fine on my own."

He didn't reply to that but said, "Let's start getting this stuff open and out. Oh, paper plates. There's a tray of plastic forks and all on the counter... We'll be ready, and if there's time..."

"If there's time, what?"

"We'll quickly run up to my office."

"Shouldn't we do that first? Food gets cold. I see you have crawfish étouffée, gumbo...all the right stuff, huh?"

"One hopes. You're right. Leave it all covered. That's a salad—doesn't matter. Come on upstairs," he said.

He hurried ahead of her, turning to the right.

His office was impressively neat and well equipped with his computer, a good-sized monitor, printer/copier complete with a scanner and a tray with neatly folded papers. His desk was large with an ergonomic chair, and there was a love seat in the rear of the room and another chair that could be brought up to the desk.

She wondered who he might work with here at times.

And she couldn't help but feel a bit of jealousy. Did

he write music sometimes? Maybe with someone…with whom he could make beautiful music?

"All right, the remaining group. Four guys—one of them my grandfather. Hank always admitted he did some pot in his day, doesn't care for it now, says he can take a nap at the drop of a hat without it. Drinking—a bit to excess in his younger days, wild, crazy and a success—but he says he respected Jake so much, even when he didn't realize it, and he learned to temper himself. Yes, he's my grandfather, and yes, I want him to be innocent."

"Did any of them go crazy on drugs at any time?" Sky murmured.

"Not really, and certainly not in comparison to a lot of groups out there who suddenly had tons of money and adulation. I looked up a bunch of public-domain stuff. They never went crazy peeing on stage à la Jim Morrison or anything, but Joe Garcia once drank himself into a stupor and ripped up a hotel room and cooled his heels in jail overnight."

"Brandon?" Sky asked.

"He's been rowdy a few times, but whatever he has or hasn't done, it was never bad enough for an arrest. I've been with him during Mardi Gras when I was worried that he'd get himself in trouble and I wanted to make sure he'd get home okay. Brandon…he was there that night."

Sky nodded. "I've never seen Mark or Chris have anything more than a beer or two. And if he does drugs of any kind, Brandon certainly has never asked me to join in. Then again, other than being polite when my mom has had anyone around, I haven't really hung out with any of these people for years."

"Your dad never frowned on anyone having a drink.

Even sober, he'd buy a beer for a friend. He'd be out of there if people were drinking to excess, they… Well, they just didn't. They respected him, and they followed his lead. They might all owe him their careers—and their lives."

"Roadies?" Skylar said.

"Okay, let's just remember we can't label them as guilty of anything just because we were never as close to any of them as we were the band members," Chase said.

Sky smiled. "Gotcha. So…?"

"So. Justin West, Charlie Bentley and Nathan Harrison," Chase said. "Justin has been with the group longest, he's turning fifty in the fall, and has no arrest record that I can find, and records like that are accessible. I have seen Justin kick back after a show with a lot of tequila, but he's also a family man, two sons in college, still married to Julia, his wife of twenty-seven years. Charlie Bentley, forty-three, divorced, handsome man, glad to sweep up the ladies after a performance. He had a DUI back in 2008. He was young, and in the biz… Driving under any kind of influence is a sin in my book—plenty of rideshare companies out there—but that's a personal thing."

"Not personal at all. Too many people have been injured or killed by impaired drivers," Sky said.

He nodded. "Still, doesn't turn him into a murderer or…"

"Drug pusher?"

"Right. Then we have Nathan Harrison. Also in his early forties, also divorced—a couple of times—still a good dad to his kids, so I hear. Coaches his son's Little League team and is on decent terms with both his ex-wives, no arrest record, but again, likes to party after a show and considers himself quite the hunk for those young women who like to hang around rock stars."

A buzzing sounded.

"First of our lunch guests," Chase said, rising. "Let's see who it is."

"Everyone responded. Hanging around until sound checks and all tonight," Sky murmured. "Well, except for Hank, of course—"

"Because Gramps is in the hospital," Chase reminded her.

"He's doing okay?"

"He'll be in there another week or so and then... He'll be out of any kind of heavy lifting until he finishes with his cardio rehab."

"Puts you in a bad position, doesn't it?" Sky asked him.

"What do you mean?"

"Skyhawk with no drummer."

"You don't hang around a lot. They have no lead singer and they've managed."

Sky laughed. "All those guys sing, and they've divided the songs well. But being a drummer...hmm, harder call."

"And the rock world is filled with them."

"But not drummers who belong with Skyhawk."

"Hey, let's focus. Be charming and fun and see what we can learn about people."

Sky nodded gravely. "Someone fixed that amp. And they knew how to do it. Fray it just enough that the band would be in the middle of something and that would mean my dad would be impatient enough to fix it himself without stopping the show."

"They're all fairly tech-savvy when it comes to the shows."

"No, seriously, think about it. There's so much going

on. The light show, the mic stands, the amplifiers, all usually run by a good DJ until the band's front man takes over. I think—"

"I think we're talking about a single wire—one mic."

She stopped, almost tripping down the stairs. She grabbed his arm to steady herself. Naturally, he was there, catching her. But she looked into his eyes.

"You knew—you knew long before all this came along. You have known that what happened to my dad wasn't an accident and—"

"I haven't known anything. I've suspected some things, yes. But don't you understand? We don't know who to suspect, and even if we did, damn it, Sky, the legal system works on proof. I don't like that you're here, because yes, I think something was done on purpose to your dad. And if whoever did it thinks you're on his trail, there's going to be another so-called accident!"

She was still holding his arm. His hands were still on her shoulders.

The buzzing sounded again.

He released her and turned and headed on down the stairs, hitting keys on his system that opened the gate and the front door.

He stepped out to the porch.

Their lunch guests were arriving.

Chapter Four

"Skylar of Skyhawk! Wow, kid, it is great to see you!"

Nathan Harrison was the first to arrive. He greeted Skylar with a massive hug, pulling her tightly into an embrace, then setting her at arm's length to study her. "Honey," he added, "you are beautiful like your mama, but man…do you have a lot of your dad in you! That dark hair and those blue, blue eyes! I'm thrilled, and I swear," he added, suddenly serious, "your daddy is going to be smiling up in heaven, knowing his girl is doing his stuff with a voice to challenge the angels!"

Nathan was a solid, strong and good-looking man with red-blond hair, a beard and a mustache that made him look like a Viking roadie. He'd always been nice to her, but she knew he could be wild.

She liked Nathan. His hug was warm. His welcome seemed real.

But then, who? She had always cared about these people, her "uncles" when Skyhawk had performed with all this crew for years and years.

"Hey!" Chase said lightly. "Watch the merchandise."

"Aw, come on! Jealous of an old man?" Nathan returned. He cast his head at an angle, arching a brow. "Hmm. You young-uns are hosting this luncheon together, I surmise?"

"Well, it's lunch, and we're both here," Sky said lightly. "Nathan, great to see you. How have you been?"

"Up to no good, like usual!"

Stepping from behind Nathan, Joe Garcia was doing the talking. He wasn't a short man, being about six feet even, but Chase and Nathan were about six three or so, making him appear small in their presence. But Joe was a showman, too. He'd kept in shape and could move like a man thirty years his junior.

He must have also been a mind reader because he quickly said, "Come on, now! The best things come in small packages!"

"There's nothing small about you," Sky assured him dryly, giving him a hug, too.

The buzz sounded again.

"That's going to be Justin and Charlie," Nathan told them. "You know, both moved out of New Orleans. Justin's living down in Orlando and Charlie headed up to Baton Rouge. The pandemic years were hard, Skyhawk wasn't performing and..."

"Hey!" Joe protested. "We kept you guys on payroll all the way through it." He looked at Sky and gave her an encouraging smile. "That was something your dad insisted on—none of the usual bonuses and perks, but a paycheck at the very least."

"And were we grateful! But in Orlando, Justin could have his family near the theme parks, and there wound up being some work down there. But you know Justin—he'd never let anything interfere with Skyhawk." He laughed suddenly. "He liked being a three- to four-hour drive to the Fort Lauderdale and Miami areas, too. 'Cause, you know, Skyhawk isn't the only group heading out there!

He took the kids down to see Cheap Trick last year, and he worked some old-timers, too. Anyway, he's super excited. Says that age doesn't dull a rocker—like Cheap Trick commanded that state. But this show has you, Sky! The Sky of Skyhawk. Sold out, you know, and resales… People are asking like crazy—in the thousands—to get in. This is going to…"

"Rock?" Chase suggested.

"We will rock it," Joe promised. "Hey, it's Itch and Scratch, Mr. Mom Justin and Wild Man, Crazy Charlie. Now, there's a pairing for you!"

Justin and Charlie came in, making faces at Joe. "Hey, Mr. Mom?" Justin demanded.

"Said with love and all good things," Joe promised him. "You managed this all being a great husband and dad."

"Hmm. Wild Man? Crazy Charlie?" Charlie asked.

Skylar had a smile plastered on her face as she accepted hugs from the two of them, too. There was nothing wrong with Justin's looks; he was a young, strong sixty-plus, but he tended to have a more serious demeanor, and she'd noted through many occasions that he was happiest when his wife was able to attend whatever gig they were working and that he worried about the right gift for her on any occasion. On the other hand, Charlie had dark brown eyes, almost platinum hair and a smile that made him alluring—except to Sky, it also made him appear a little… smarmy. If that was a word.

"You are a wild man," Joe said simply. "But hey—"

"Hey, yeah, the invitation came from Sky's email—to come to Chase's house. So, hmm, should we assume some old fires have rekindled and we have a hunk, a hunk of burning love going on here?" Charlie asked.

"Charlie," Joe murmured. "The kids..."

"Kids? Joe, they grew up!" Justin protested.

"My question is purely selfish. If the studly drummer is occupied with the luscious young singer, that leaves more adoring fans ready to pounce on a roadie just because he's close to the band!" Charlie said.

Sky smiled and said, "Thank you. I think. Yeah, um, I mean, who knows? But...yes...we're having this luncheon together."

"You two are together?" Joe said, looking at them. He seemed surprised at first and then pleased. "Jake would be pleased," Joe said softly. "Chase is a good boy—"

"Joe! These *kids* are both over twenty-one now and, from what I hear, leading full and responsible lives," Nathan said, stepping back into the conversation. "Then again," he added with a shrug, "you guys will be kids to Joe and the other oldsters as long as we all live."

"True," Chase said, setting his arm around Sky's shoulders. "Guess what, Nathan. Hank calls you guys *kids*, too. He told me he used to call anyone under forty a kid, but now it's anyone under fifty."

"We're going to miss Hank," Joe said. "But! We want him better. The world is revolving again, and we've gotten so many offers."

"And," Charlie said, "let's hope you're going to take them. Have to stay relevant. I mean, we may all know you, Chris and Mark are older than dirt, but between us all, we caught some great acts last year! I saw the Stones, still amazing. I saw the Eagles, Def Leppard, U2 and more, but I believe putting the *Sky* into Skyhawk is going to be something amazing!"

"Hey," Chris protested, "I may be older than dirt, but I

have a full head of hair, dark bedroom eyes—if I do say so myself—and I can pass for...well, at least five years younger. Neither here nor there. Back to it. So... Sky?"

"I can't promise a tour," Sky told him.

"But she's not *not* promising a tour, either," Chase said.

"Well, cool, young McCoy. We believe Hank will be back," Joe said, "but we all know you're welcome for half the gig anytime."

"Hey—and there, at the gate. Mark, Chris and Brandon!" Sky said.

Sky wanted this lunch; they needed the gathering. Or did they? Was it going to help any? They knew the players... Nathan, reserved, glad to be behind the curtain. Charlie, always out there, the guy to overdo things.

But did that make him...homicidal?

But something *had* happened. Chase had always known it; he had been working it, and maybe what had happened had turned him onto the path he'd taken as what now seemed to be the life of a perpetual student.

And she felt uncomfortable, standing there as they were.

"Hail, hail! The gang's all here!"

"You're here," Mark said, looking from Nathan to Charlie to Justin. "You're here. But tonight, we have our chance at the venue—"

"Are you kidding, man?" Justin asked. "We started last night, and we finished up this morning. All we need is Skyhawk up on the stage."

"Sky and Skyhawk!" Charlie said, turning to look at her. His expression was serious, and his words were spoken with what seemed like real warmth. "Seriously, Sky. Your dad was always so proud of you. On stage and off. Someone asked him once what he wanted you to be when you grew up—a rock star, or maybe president of the United States. He said he just wanted you to grow up to be a good and decent person doing what you loved for a living, whatever that proved to be. He would be so proud."

"Charlie," she said softly, "thank you. That's very sweet of you." She turned to the others. "Come on, we've provided all kinds of our city's finest choices. I mean we are a music city, and we are a food city! Let's eat! We have jambalaya, crawfish étouffée and so much more! Let's do this!"

"Fine!" Chris said. "Boy, and it's as if he heard the dinner bell—here comes Brandon now!"

Chase moved ahead and did a presentation of all the dishes he had ordered, with Chris Wiley laughing and telling him it was a feast for kings—on paper plates.

"I have important work tonight. No time for dishes," Chase explained. "Eight chairs at the table, but we can drag in the stools from the kitchen, or anyone can sit wherever they want to sit. Just dig in. It's great to be together."

"Let's do a video chat with Hank, too, huh? Could we?" Mark asked.

"Sure, he has his phone," Chase said. "I'll try to reach him."

He stepped into the kitchen area to make the call while the others grabbed plates and piled them high.

Sky waited for the others and realized she was standing back. To her surprise, Charlie turned to her and spoke softly. "Sky…"

"Yes?"

He looked pained. "I…I know how to work a stage. I know we weren't blamed, and the fire marshal said there was a faulty wire, no one could have done anything. I just… I always felt guilty. As if there should have been something…that I should have seen something, that…"

"Charlie, stop, please!" she said, setting an arm on his shoulder. He was the wild one. The one who might have gone off the deep end at one time or another.

But she believed he was sincere. His eyes were filled with pain.

"Charlie, I know that you know wires, and I know you'd never have allowed anything bad up there. I know you loved my dad. Please, the pain of loss is bad enough. We never blamed you, my mom never blamed you."

"Thank you," he said quietly. "I appreciate your words. They help."

"Got him!" Chase said, walking back in from the kitchen. He lifted his phone. Hank was there in his hospital bed, but Sky was relieved to see that despite his recent health scare, he looked good. Full head of snow-white hair, handsome face betraying his years and a smile that was still great. She imagined after many years had passed Chase by, he might look much the same.

"Hey!" Hank greeted the others. "Get out there tonight and knock 'em—"

He broke off. Of course he'd been about to say *knock 'em dead.*

But no one in Skyhawk was going to use that expression.

"Knock 'em off their feet! Rock the house down. I can't be there," Hank said, "but in my mind, your substitute may be the better choice."

"Never, Gramps," Chase told him. "But I'll do my best."

"Sky, you look stunning! Then again, always," Hank told her.

"Thanks, Hank. And you feel better soon. You are still one handsome devil!" she assured him.

"I wish I was there for the food."

"Soon enough, Gramps," Chase said sternly. "You're going to follow the doctors'—"

"Orders, yes, Chase, I promise. Because if Skyhawk is hitting the tour circuit along with a lot of our fellows from the seventies and eighties, I'm going to be well and hitting it with everyone again. Nathan, Justin, Charlie—great that you're on it. Where's whatshisname?" Hank asked suddenly.

"Gramps, who is whatshisname?" Chase asked.

"You are talking about Malcolm—Kenneth Malcolm?" Nathan asked.

"Yeah. He's still working the place, right?" Hank asked.

"Oh, yeah," Mark said. "Sorry, I thought I'd mentioned that when I visited to tell you we'd been to the place."

"His name was on the paperwork when we made the plans," Hank said. "Months ago. Didn't know, though, with the way things go these days—"

"Oh, yeah, he's still there. And guess what? He's been really decent," Charlie told him. "I think he had tickets and the thing is sold out and he's raking it in on resale."

"Whatever, as long as it all goes well. Sky, I swear, I dreamed about being on a cloud with your dad watching, and he was beaming," Hank said.

"Thanks, Hank," Sky told him.

"And get the video chick or whoever is on doing the Jumbotrons to make sure she's got me on the wire while it's going on!" Hank said.

"Will do, Gramps," Chase promised.

"Go eat!" Hank commanded. "Oh, wait. I can see Mark and Joe chewing. But the rest of you—have lunch! I can almost smell it from here. They have me on a cruel diet—yeah, yeah, yeah, I promise I'm going to stick to it! But go—quit torturing me, showing it all to me."

"Bye, Hank, just get well," Charlie said, and his words were echoed around the room.

Chase ended the video call.

"We never answered him," Joe said. "Did you guys invite Kenneth Malcolm?"

Chase made a face. "I didn't think of him."

"Neither did I," Sky admitted.

"He's a jerk anyway," Justin said with a shrug. "He's being nice because he's making money. Doesn't matter—I'm still glad to be away from him for this. Tonight, during tech, he'll be all over us, I promise you. So… Gumbo! I love it!"

Food and good humor went all around, different band members and stage techs sitting next to each other, switching around for dessert—bread pudding and pecan pie—and exchanging seats again.

Then Justin glanced at his watch. "Let's get over there. We've a host of other people working under us on this. The MC, the light crew, the computer geek…and because of Mr. Kenneth Malcolm, I'd love to see it all go right."

"We're out of here!" Nathan agreed. "Charlie, come on. We're aiming for perfect!"

"Nothing is ever perfect," Joe warned.

"But we gotta aim high, right?" Mark asked, studying Sky. "Aim high, like our founder, but now we've got his daughter, and…"

Chase slipped his arms around Sky, pulling her back against him as he spoke over her shoulders. "Jake's beautiful Sky, as perfect as we can get, right?"

"No, no, no, no, no—not putting it all on me!" Sky said lightly. "Anyway, thank you, guys, all of you. This was great."

"No, thank you and Chase, our legacy, eh?" Chris offered.

"Aw, chopped liver over here?" Brandon asked, causing them all to laugh.

"Prime sirloin," Mark assured him. "And Chris is bringing you in a lot for this one, right?"

"Oh, yeah. Hey, when time starts going by, well… It's nice to see you've passed on something of value—and whether you kids decide to keep at it or not, you made us feel good, so…prime sirloin!"

"Personally, I was thinking of filet," Sky said, smiling at Brandon. He grinned in return.

"So we'll meet up again in a few hours," Mark said. "After last night, I have nothing but faith. Oh, for the performance, we'll have the ballad as the encore. And maybe—the encore should have at least two numbers—we'll also do 'Real Paradise.'"

"Gotcha," Chase assured him.

One by one, their guests filed out. When they were gone, Chase was silent.

"Well, did you get anything?" she asked him.

"Charlie would have been first on my list," Chase said. "And no more."

"Really?" Sky pressed. "I mean…he's…he was super and kind, but he is the one most likely to fall to excess."

Chase let out a long sigh. "Okay. We both think it was

more than an accident. That means that your dad was going to do something after the show that involved someone—who or what, we don't know. He didn't care if other people had their minor vices, but…"

"He'd care if someone was selling drugs," Sky said.

"And those who use recreationally—sometimes a little too recreationally—aren't usually the ones with the control to make money on the scam."

"So…why?" Sky asked, perplexed. "Skyhawk started off in a garage, and they all struggled. But then they got hot, and everyone involved made money. Why—"

Chase frowned. "I don't know. I've deep-dived into the financials—"

"What?" Sky interrupted explosively.

"Hey, years of criminology courses can pay off," he said lightly. "We have a few hours—"

"Dog," Skylar said.

"What did you say?" he demanded.

She smiled. "You said I needed a dog. Let's head to the pound."

He was quiet for a minute and then looked at her, a half grin on his lips. "We can get a dog. You should have one. A dog is always good. But you won't get rid of me. Not until—"

"Until we get through this? Because," she added, frustrated, "we never got any answers."

"But we will," he assured her. "Still, a dog. A big one with a bark that shakes the very trees."

"No Teacup Yorkies or the like, eh?" she said lightly. "What if a big dog is mean—"

"Wait!" he said. "I have the perfect dog. Let me get this

all cleaned up, and then I have a friend you should meet. Great guy, with great, perfect dogs."

"I thought I was going to adopt a dog that needed a home."

"You'll be adopting. Wait and see. I've got the ticket on this one."

He turned away from her, taking out trash bags. She hopped in to help him, separating trash from recycling. They were quickly done, and he swore he'd be right down as he ran quickly up the stairs.

"Let's go," he said, descending almost as rapidly as he had left.

"Okay. Where are we heading?"

"Tremé," he told her. "A great piece of property there… well, you'll see!"

They headed out, leaving the French Quarter to cross Rampart. In a few minutes, they came to a solid block that seemed to be mainly pasture and stables.

"Someone who owns a carriage company?" Sky asked.

"No, Trey owns horses, but not carriage horses. He's just a friend who…lectured one day. He's retired now and came into some family money."

Chase spoke as he pulled into a parking space outside a wooden fence. They had barely gotten out of the car when a gate opened and an older man appeared, a welcoming smile on his face.

"Chase!" he said with pleasure.

"Trey!" Chase called in return, and leading Sky forward, he introduced her and then said, "Sky, this is Trey Montgomery, and I think we might just call him an animal whisperer since he has enormous talents with all kinds of creatures!"

"Come in, come in, and welcome!" Trey said. He was almost Chase's height and, though lean, seemed to be made of sinewy muscles.

"Retired—teacher?" she asked him.

"Something like that," he told her. "I sure love what I do now, though." He pointed out a pasture where five horses were wandering about, snatching bits of grass here and there from the earth. "The paint there—that's Sally. She just came in last week." He paused, shrugging. "Most workhorses are tended to carefully, fed, seen by the vet… then you hit an idiot who should never be around any kind of animal—including humankind—and he abuses a creature to no end. We've finally taken care of the sores in her mouth from having a bridle ripped around like a hockey puck, and she lets me approach her. I don't think we'll ever see her coat grow back over some of the scars she got from a whip, but…hey, at least they got the bastard on animal-abuse charges!"

"And you got the horse," Chase said, smiling.

"Sally already comes to me," Trey said happily. "But you don't want a horse. You want a dog. I think I have the perfect new friend. Come on to the house!"

His house was a simple ranch-style dwelling; when Trey opened the door, he was greeted by a bevy of dogs, most of them German shepherds or shepherd mixes. He made a point of petting them all, as did Chase and then Skylar.

"So…" Chase said.

"Larry," Trey said. "Right there. He's a shepherd/Lab mix, a big boy, trained in all kinds of disciplines, and doing great since he has been with me. He was injured on the job and retired."

"Injured—" Sky began.

"He was a police dog, worked with the canine squad," Chase explained.

"And he's already taken to you!" Trey said happily.

He had, Sky realized. The dog they called Larry was by her side, wagging his tail as he looked up at her. He looked mostly like a shepherd, but his coloring was golden Lab. He was a handsome creature, and his tail kept wagging away as he stood by her side.

"Think Larry chose you!" Trey said.

"Sky?" Chase asked.

"I—uh—I think Larry is great. I just worry—as Chase knows—because I travel on business—"

"Larry is welcome back here whenever you need to go. As you can see, I have ample room. So can I get you kids some coffee or anything? Have you had lunch?"

"Enough lunch to last forever," Chase said. "Thanks, Trey. We have to get to the tech rehearsal, too, so—"

"And you did get me tickets?" Trey said.

"Oh, you bet," Chase affirmed.

"His collar is on him. I'll get his papers," Trey said. "Happy dog, happy owner!"

Sky blinked, looking at Chase. She realized her hand was still on Larry's soft head. She had always loved dogs—it had just seemed too cruel to own one and board it every other minute.

But this…

He was an amazing dog, and one that came with boarding when necessary?

"What are you, a magician, or friends with half the city?" Sky asked Chase.

He shrugged. "I've met a few people along the way. We'll get Larry to my place and—"

"Hey! My dog, my place," Sky said.

"Okay, but—"

"Right. You're not leaving me. You'll spend another night crinkled up on the couch."

"You got it," he told her.

She let out a frustrated sigh. "Knock yourself out, then."

"It's getting late. Onward to your house. And you don't have to worry about him being housebroken—all of Trey's pups are."

"Naturally. What other magic tricks do you have up your sleeve?"

Trey returned, bringing her Larry's vet papers and license information…and a bag of dog food.

"Thought I'd get you started out right," he told Sky. "And I'm glad you like him. Looks like Larry has truly chosen you."

Sky thanked him, still a little amazed she'd been the one to remind Chase he'd suggested she get a dog.

And he'd found her Larry—housebroken, trained, loving—so quickly.

Chase thanked Trey who told him he was thrilled Larry was going to such a good home. In a few minutes, they were on their way.

He shrugged, ushering Larry into the back seat of his car. She slid into the passenger's seat. Larry took a seat without protest. Naturally, he was well behaved in the car as well.

They drove in silence to Sky's house. "Give him some water and a bowl of food, and he'll be fine until we're back," Chase said.

"Okay."

"I'll wait in the car. We want to be on time."

He stayed in the car on the street. Sky keyed in the gate and the front door and led Larry in. "Larry," she told the dog, "I didn't know I needed a dog, but you're pretty darned cool, and I hope you like this place and… I don't really care if you get on the couch." She laughed suddenly, rubbing the dog's head. "Get lots of hair on it for that guy out in the car. I want to see the two of you sleep on that thing!"

Larry barked and wagged his tail.

She quickly found bowls for water and food and assured the dog she'd be back. He curled up on the kitchen floor, and she could almost swear that he nodded.

Then she left the house, reassuring herself that the door and the gate were securely locked.

"Ready?" he asked as she slid back into her seat.

"Well, I'm here. And Larry is sleeping on the kitchen floor. Hey, who names a dog Larry?" she mused.

"You don't like it? I guess you could rename him."

"Larry is fine," she said, looking out the window as they drove through the city she'd known all her life, a city she loved.

The city her dad had loved so much.

"You okay?" he asked her.

"Yep. Except…"

"You're frustrated. And it's okay. We're here. Just… act normal."

"Right. *Normal*."

Parking by the doors had been arranged for the band, and it was easy to reach the backstage doors. As they stepped around in the wings, Sky saw the crew was already rehearsing with the lights. Hundreds of lights were spread about the stage and the massive audience. They turned to various shades of blue, pink, orange, yellow and purple.

"It's fantastic, and wait until you see the spotlights going and everything up on the Jumbotrons!" said Justin, who was adjusting the levels on the giant soundboard.

"Can't finish that setup until I have the band all here," he said. "And if there's a problem, I'll be right there in the wings, ready to run on out. I'm going to be switching out the mics and the instruments when needed, too."

"Thanks, Justin. We're the first?" Chase asked.

"No!" Mark Reynolds said, hurrying in from the opposite wing. "I was just talking to Kenneth Malcolm, assuring him we'll be perfect with two techs, more than we've had a dozen times in the last decades. But…this is his place, so…"

"Sky!"

She heard her name called and turned to see Kenneth Malcolm was coming out. He was smiling broadly, ready to greet her.

She forced a smile to her lips.

He drew her into a hug instantly, and she tried not to stiffen, tried to return his touch. He drew back, a man like the roadies, somewhere between forty and fifty, lean and sharp with a full head of neatly combed dark hair and light gray eyes. And, always—always—the businessman, wearing a perfectly tailored suit.

"I can't tell you how delighted we are that you're here. I know you've avoided the spotlight, but people see it as extra special that you're doing your dad's numbers. He was such a showman, writer, guitarist, vocalist…talker! You're going to talk to the audience, too, I hope."

Sky glanced at Chase.

"Oh, she can talk!" Chase said.

"Oh, Chase, cool, welcome, and I can't tell you how glad we are that you're here, subbing for Hank. How's he doing?"

"Great. He'll be back to it all very soon," Chase said.

"When you can't have all of Skyhawk, it's amazing to have a Skyhawk legacy!" Malcolm said. "Seriously—"

"Ah, there's Joe!" Chase said. "We can get this started, and thanks, the venue looks terrific—"

"We have a great staff here, and they've worked great with Skyhawk's guys," Malcolm said. "I'm out of here—or out into the audience. I want to see all that's going on tonight, make sure… Well, you know, tomorrow night, I'll be dealing with all kinds of stuff, so…"

"Great to see you, and thank you," Sky murmured, noting that Chris and Brandon had come in and Justin was talking to them.

"Ready to get some sound checks going!" Mark called.

Brandon walked up to her with a guitar. "One of your dad's," he told her.

She thanked him. He headed to the side, saying that everyone had everything.

Before he walked to the drums, Chase paused by her.

"You okay for this part?" he asked her.

She nodded. "I… Yeah. Probably not so much talking tonight—"

"Tonight is sound and light check. Channel Jake tomorrow night," he said, lightly touching her hair.

"Ready to go. List is up on the screen right now!" Mark called.

Sky held her father's guitar. She closed her eyes tightly

for a moment, and a sad smile came to her lips. Jake would be glad to see her there.

If only the cloud wasn't there, gray and creating something over it all…

But minutes later, after the first numbers, she let her fears, her anger, her loss and her pain all go. She thought of the amazing artists she had seen just walking down the streets of New Orleans, artists who would have given just about anything for the chance Jake had given her, the chance to do what she loved on such a stage.

No matter what, music and family had been Jake Ferguson's life.

And she would give his music everything that she had within her.

The spotlight fell on her, and there seemed to be a hush despite the music as she sang—and channeled Jake.

She did talk. She introduced the drum solo, spotlighted each member of the band, drew Brandon out from the sidelines and had him play and sing with her.

She heard the others come in on the harmonies, Chase pick up on the duets. And always, the lights glimmered around her.

She realized she could compartmentalize what they were doing…

They would get to the truth.

But she would do the show, too, with all of her heart, in memory of the man she had loved. And in doing so, she took a minute between the songs to just talk about her father, about the amazing man he had been…

And it was good.

There was a silence following her words as she prepared to say goodbye so they could walk off—and then, of course, return for the encore they believed the audience would demand.

Then there was applause, real and spontaneous, from the band members, the crew, everyone out adjusting lights and screens and everything else that would go with the show.

“Thank you!” she cried. “And Skyhawk thanks you! Good night!”

She and the others headed off.

Charlie, Justin and Nathan were there, nodding to her, beaming, each congratulating her and Chase and Brandon.

“Now, let it go a few beats and then…everyone back out!” Mark said.

They headed out and did the last two numbers.

“If only the real show goes so remarkably!” Joe Garcia said, grinning. “Sky, thanks, that was… Man, your dad is grinning from ear to ear up in heaven!”

Sky thanked him.

“Hey, you are joining us for a quick drink tonight, right?” Brandon asked. “You said you would!”

“Um, well, I was going to, but today I got a dog—”

“Cool. Dogs are cool,” Brandon said. “But come on, another thirty minutes. There’s a great quiet place in the Irish Channel, and we can slip away for just a few minutes!”

“Sure,” Chase said, sliding up behind her and slipping an arm around her. “Sky, come on, let’s hang for just a bit.”

She looked at him, a question in her eyes. He didn’t have to nod. She almost smiled. There had been times in the past when…

She was feeling that now. That sense of both security and sensuality when he touched her.

Compartmentalize! she reminded herself.

But that night, it seemed they were joining the crowd.

"Sure," she said.

"Hey, guys! Barbie and Ken are coming with us!" Brandon called. "Drinks on us after that great lunch."

"Snacks, too—no dinner tonight," Chase said. He frowned suddenly, and she realized his phone was vibrating as he reached into a pocket to retrieve it.

"A sec, guys. I'm right with you."

He stepped away for a minute. Sky smiled at Brandon as he called out to the others, finding out who was driving with who.

Chase stepped back up by her and put his arm around her shoulders again.

Something about him had changed. Others wouldn't notice.

But she had once known him oh so well.

"We're going to take my car—probably a quick drink and then out of there. New dog, remember? Anyway, see you there," he said to the others.

There was a lot of tension in his touch. He led her out through the back. Quickly.

"What's wrong?" she asked him as they reached the car.

He shook his head. He wasn't speaking; maybe there were ears somewhere near them.

Skylar crawled into the car and waited.

Once he had gunned the engine and they were moving, she turned to him. "Chase! What the hell is going on?"

Chapter Five

Chase kept his eyes on the road and sighed inwardly. He hated lying, and yet he'd spent a whole two days with Skylar. Intense days that, when he touched her, seemed to wash away the years.

But she had turned away from him. And he wasn't in a position now to bare his heart—and his life—to her.

"Call from a friend," he said.

"And?"

"They had a death down by the river," he said. "A kid… it was just marijuana. College kid, with friends, took a few puffs…seized and was dead. The only good thing is that watching him freaked out his friends and none of them touched the stuff after that… It's headed to a lab. But sounds like the weed had been contaminated with fentanyl. Apparently, it's a huge problem now, pills, uppers, downers, weed, cocaine…tons of drugs contaminated."

"Wow. That's horrible. And your friend called you?"

"It's all over the news."

"Right. But the friend called you," she pressed.

He turned to look at her briefly and then quickly returned his attention to the road. He didn't have to look at Sky to see her face in his mind's eye. Eyes bluer than the bluest sky, hair like her dad's, dark as ink, flowing around her shoulders. He'd fallen in love with her when he was young. And in all the years that had gone by…

He'd been practical. She was gone. He'd met people. But he hadn't had a real relationship since they'd been together. Young Chase had believed they'd eventually marry, that some people were lucky in life and they met someone who was there for them for the rest of their lives.

"Chase?"

"Yeah?"

She let out a loud sigh of exasperation. "Chase! Friends call you to report the news? Why? What is going on?"

He shrugged. "Hey. We're with a rock band. Everyone knows rock and roll may lead us all to some kind of excess," he said sarcastically.

"Chase—"

"Oh, come on! You know what? I'm scared to death for you, and I need to trust you right now. And I'm not really sure how to deal with either."

"Why wouldn't you trust me?"

"Oh, I don't know. Never returning a call, email or text. Pretending as if I'd fallen off the face of the earth—"

"Chase, I couldn't deal! I just couldn't deal, and I… Look, I'm sorry! But you're the one scared to death for me, so please, let me in on whatever the hell it is that's going on," she pleaded.

"You know what's going on," he said quietly. "This whole thing has to do with drugs. And I think someone involved—close, at the very least—has been involved with some very bad drugs that have been going around. Yeah, I have friends. You do, too. The old couple next to you with the dog—Tim Hanson and his wife, Liz. I know you are friends with them. Oh, I also know you like to sing sometimes at Jazz Mass."

"What? Wait! Have you been—"

"Did I try to follow you a bit and make sure you were moving on all right with your life? Yeah, I did. I cared. Sue me. But now…"

"Now, yeah, I got it. Bad drugs are out there. My father might have known something. And so he died, because he wouldn't let innocent people be harmed by others. And despite being clean, he didn't care if someone had a joint or a beer, but he would have been furious if—"

"If," Chase finished, "someone was out there purposely trying to addict the youth of America or, worse, to kill innocents, your dad would have acted. Because the big players out there up the profits in drugs by cutting them big-time. As in with fentanyl."

"So," she said slowly, "someone out there knows you believe someone in or around Skyhawk is doing this? You have some interesting friends."

"Well, of course I do!" he said. "You know I've worked in labs, and I've taken all kinds of classes in criminology."

"Are you sure they are all friends?" she asked.

He groaned. "I got a call from a friend, yes. A trusted friend."

"How do you know them?" she asked.

He was going to have to tell her at least something of the truth. But first, they had reached the bar where they were supposed to meet the others. He found street parking, turned off the car and sat for a minute.

"Because my friend is someone I met at a lecture. And he's with the FBI."

"Oh," she said simply. "Well, that's good, right? Is this friend going to be coming to the concert?"

"Yes," he admitted.

"That's cool," she murmured, looking down at her hands. Then she turned to him. "Though, neither of us is going to be electrocuted. The guys made a point of saying anything to do with electric or sound or even lights, they'd be handling it."

He nodded and turned and said fiercely, "And that's for real. You don't touch anything. Anything at all. Promise!"

"Of course. But you have to promise me the same."

"I do, of course. But the drummer isn't the front man—or woman. You are."

"I promise. Should we go in?" Sky asked.

He nodded. "Yeah. But..."

"But?"

"You don't drink anything that I don't give you, okay?"

"Now you want me to worry about drinks? In a bar that's been here forever?"

Chase didn't get a chance to answer. He saw Joe Garcia was on the sidewalk, hurrying toward them and tapping at Sky's window.

He indicated that they were getting out, and he and Sky exited from their respective sides of the car.

"Chase, Sky," Joe said excitedly, "this is a cool happenstance. A reporter from *the* major music magazine is in the bar—recognized me and Mark—and is dying to interview Sky!"

"Oh, well, I'm not—"

"Honey, please. No, it's not like we're hurting, like we won't survive, but anytime something like that goes around, songs are played and played on the radio and… Please, it will only take a few minutes, I promise!"

Sky glanced over at Chase and he nodded. "I'll be right there," he promised.

"Okay, um, sure, if it helps everyone, then…sure."

They headed back in together. It was a neighborhood kind of place—not like a bar on Bourbon Street, blasting music and catering to tourists. It was somewhat surprising that a reporter had made his way here, but when Joe introduced him and Sky to the man, it turned out his name was Jimmy Broussard. He had been born in New Orleans but headed out to California for work. Naturally, he latched on anytime he could when a known band was playing in the vicinity.

Broussard was maybe in his late thirties, and despite the fact he'd probably interviewed dozens of music celebrities, he seemed in awe of Sky. He shook her hand, telling her she looked like her father and added quickly, "A beautiful, feminine version of your dad, of course."

She thanked him and glanced a little nervously at Chase.

"The two of them are a thing," Joe said. "If you want Sky—"

"Please, Chase, join us!" Broussard said. He pointed to a table at the back of the bar. It was quiet there; music was playing, but it wasn't a live band. It was controlled from behind the bar and was kept at a volume that allowed for conversation.

"Sky, Chase, what would you like—" Joe began.

"No, not to worry. I know what she likes," Chase said. "Mr. Broussard?"

"I'm good, got a beer," Broussard said.

Chase hurried to the bar himself and asked for two beers—in bottles. He brought them back to the table where Broussard was smiling at Sky as they waited.

"Thanks," Sky murmured.

"Broussard, you're sure—"

"Got my beer right here, never go for more than one. Anyway..." he turned to Sky as Chase took a seat at the table "...I just loved your dad's work," he told her. "You know, some songs are catchy just because you've got a beat that people can't resist. Words don't even matter—it's the tune. A tune that makes you move, that is just peppy. But so many of the groups from decades past had some real songwriters in them, too," he told her.

She smiled at him in turn. She seemed okay with the reporter, which was good on many fronts.

"Yeah," she said. "My dad loved what he called the storytellers. He was a big fan of Roger Waters and Pink Floyd. The Who and Pete Townshend with *Tommy*, the rock opera...there were a lot of great writers out there, really. And there still are! Music keeps growing. Oh, that was something else my dad taught me. Every genre has good music, just as every genre has music that will fade. He told me one time that rap really wasn't his favorite form of music but that there was good rap and that you could combine all kinds of music. He and my mom got to see *Hamilton*, and he fell in love with it and Lin-Manuel Miranda. He was one of those guys who truly appreciated the talents of others."

"So I heard," Broussard said. "He's also known for helping young musicians—and anyone who needed help, really."

"He had a lot of pet charities. I try to keep up with them, as does my mom."

"That's great. I mean, growing up with that kind of a rock legend..."

"He was a great father. He taught me good lessons for life. I didn't get away with anything—"

Broussard laughed. "Can't imagine Jake Ferguson spanking his kid. Did you spend a lot of time in time-out?"

She shook her head. "I was a good kid. There was something about him and my mom. I wasn't afraid of horrible things happening if I misbehaved, I just didn't want to disappoint anyone."

"Wow. Great. And what about you?"

"What about me?"

"Sorry. I'm usually a great interviewer, right on with questions. I'm in awe. Anyway, what about you? Favorite group, singer—"

"I couldn't pick a favorite. If I'm looking to some of the artists from past decades... Freddie Mercury, amazing vocals. Roy Orbison! Hmm, oh, wow, Nancy Wilson from Heart. My God, what a voice! There are others, of course, so many...and..."

Broussard laughed. "It's an amazing world. Glad to be on the sidelines, though..." He paused, grinning. "My dad was an attorney. Loved boats, and we took a lot of holidays down in the Caribbean. He ran into a fellow at a local place where people just sat all together. Started talking to the fellow next to him who said he was a guitarist. My dad told him that he could help him get a real job. Turned out the fellow was Eric Clapton, possibly the best guitarist out there!" He turned to Chase suddenly. "Wow.

I'm sorry, didn't mean to be ignoring you. You are...Hank McCoy's grandson, right?"

"I am," Chase said. "And don't worry about ignoring me at all. No problem."

"Hey, drums are a big deal. And I've heard you. This is off the record—better vocals from you than your granddad, but...hey, who am I to judge?"

Sky was gazing at Chase, and he caught her eyes, and they both laughed. "A guy who has listened to more rock bands than anyone can possibly imagine?" Chase said lightly. "Anyway, I take any and all compliments. Back to Sky."

"You still play. You still sing."

"I like life low-key," she told him.

"So—kids and Jazz Mass."

"You do your homework," Chase told him.

"It's my life!" Broussard said lightly. "Anyway, Sky, thank you. I was in love with your father's talent. I think this is going to be an amazing gig."

"You'll be there?" Sky asked him.

"Oh, you bet. Hey, can I get a shot of the two of you together?"

Chase noticed Sky seemed to miss a beat, but she was quickly back with the plan.

"Of course!" Chase said quickly.

"Of course," she echoed.

They'd been sitting in chairs at a square table. Chase stood and walked around behind Sky, ducking down with an arm around her and his head by hers.

Broussard said, "Well, should have had my photographer here, but this was truly happenstance, so... Well, they say phones take incredible pictures these days."

"Any device can only take what it sees," Sky murmured.

"It sees pure beauty!" Broussard said, snapping his pic. "And handsomeness, of course," he told Chase.

Chase laughed aloud at that one. "Hey, how about 'the group at play at home'— This is where Skyhawk began years ago in a little garage," he reminded Broussard.

"Yeah, cool!" Broussard said.

The others—including roadies Nathan, Justin and Charlie—were at one of the long plank tables. Chase motioned to them and they scrambled, half the table heading to stand behind the other half, allowing room at one end for Chase and Sky.

The picture was taken.

When several backup shots had been made, Broussard thanked them all, as they did him and he was gone and the bartender-owner, Danny Murphy, came over to express his appreciation.

"The real deal. You guys are the real deal!" he told them. "And Sky…wow. Thanks. I mean, thanks. What that will do for this place… Major league!"

"Yeah, but keep it real, okay, huh?" Joe Garcia begged. "That's why we love to come here, it's just…real. Not a gig, just a beer!"

"Oh, always," Murphy promised.

"Anyway, we're going to get home—" Chase began.

"No! Hey, we're all just finally together!" Brandon protested. He went silent, though, suddenly. There was a TV screen behind the bar. A twenty-four hour news show was on and the headlines were running.

"Oh, my God!" Joe said.

"Another one," Mark added, shaking his head. "Man, am I glad I'm not young anymore."

"You'd think, too, that kids would cool it right now! I mean that poor kid, from what I'm seeing, he was just going to have few tokes!" Chris Wiley said. He looked at Brandon. "Don't even think about buying any weed right now!"

"I'm here, with you, drinking a near beer, Pops!" Brandon protested. "Not to worry. What the hell kind of a dealer does that?" he added. "Kills their customers?"

"Some ass who doesn't know that overcutting stuff to make bigger bucks doesn't do the trick. Man, that's right… poor kid," Mark said. "We haven't had trouble like this in a while now. What a…well, what a mess and a tragedy."

"Absolute tragedy," Charlie agreed, standing. He shook his head. "What is the matter with people? I'm almost glad Jake isn't here. He'd be so upset over…"

His voice trailed, and he looked at Sky. "I'm so sorry."

"It's okay. My dad would be furious, you're right," Sky said. She looked around at them all. "Everyone should be furious. This is random murder for profit. But the cops get on to people eventually. And I hope whoever did this is charged with murder."

"They'll get them. They always do," Joe said, nodding his head sagely.

"But they don't, do they?" Brandon asked, looking at Chase. "Hey, you're the guy who has taken all the classes. They don't get them all the time, do they? I mean, look at the serial killers who were out there for years and years—and those who were never caught."

"Most of the time, from the lectures I've heard, criminals eventually make mistakes," Chase said. "Any of us who might want to take a puff now and then…wouldn't be doing it right now! Hey, one more round of bottled beers. We'll play everything safe!"

He headed to the bar, keeping his eye on the table. They all seemed perplexed, horrified by what they had seen on the news.

And yet one of them…

He snatched a tray off the bar to carry the beers back, placing them in front of everyone.

"Hey, cool," Chris Wiley said, smiling at Chase. "When all else fails, you can be a bartender!"

"Aw, he's aiming higher than that!" Mark said. "What are you going to do with all these classes? You know, I just never saw you working in a basement lab, kid!"

Chase shrugged. "Thanks to you guys, I get to be whatever I want." He laughed. "Never worked in a basement. Most labs would be underwater soon in this area!"

They all laughed. Mark, Joe and Chris, the remaining original members of Skyhawk, all seemed to be at ease. Older men, those who might have retired in another life, but all still strong and vibrant. Chase was grateful his grandfather, Hank, would soon regain his strength, and he would still be part of what he had loved all his life again. And still…

Brandon? Wild child? Sometimes what was in plain sight was the simple answer.

But for some reason, Chase just didn't think it could be that easy. Gut reaction. A man's gut could be wrong.

But it could also be right.

Then…the roadies. Charlie, like Brandon, the wild child in the group. Justin, a man who by all appearances loved his wife of years and years and his sons, both in college, one headed for a career in medicine, the other in banking.

Nathan...divorced. A few times. But a man who coached his one son's team, a guy who seemed to love his children...

"I think it's time, children, that we do get back. Last tech tomorrow, and then show goes up at eight!" Mark said. He looked around the table, grimacing. "I am the oldest dude in this fizzy party now, so children, all of you—off to bed for a good night tomorrow!"

They all stood and headed out. Chase paused on the sidewalk.

"Chase?" Sky asked softly.

"Such a beautiful night!" he said.

"Yes, it is," she agreed. "For...for most of us."

"Let's get to the car. Get some sleep."

He nodded. The street here, off the tourist path and in a neighborhood section of the city, was quiet. His car was just down a block or so, and they started for it in silence.

Maybe it was the quiet, maybe it was his training, but he heard someone slip almost silently down the street toward them just as he opened the driver's door to his car.

He spun around, almost reaching for the small sidearm in its holster at his waistband which was hidden by the jacket he was wearing.

But again, gut sense had kicked in.

It was Brandon Wiley, looking at him anxiously.

"Brandon?"

"Sorry, sorry, I didn't mean to sneak up on you. I mean, I wanted to get to you without anyone else seeing... I, man, I don't know. Well, I mean, you do know. I swear, no hard drugs, but I do some weed now and then, and now..."

"Do you have something on you?" Chase asked. "Brandon—"

"Yes, yes, I do. And I don't know, Chase, I mean no one really understands what you're up to all the time, but I thought that—"

"Brandon, yeah, I know some people, and I can—"

"Please, please, please, I'm going to be sitting in for many of the numbers tomorrow night, and it all means a lot to me. I don't want to get in any trouble—"

"Brandon," Chase promised, "I'm not going to get you into any trouble. I'm going to be grateful as all hell you came to me if the stuff you have turns out to be tainted. Thing is, if there is something… Brandon, we have to know where you got it."

Brandon nodded. "I didn't buy it. There's a guy who works the spotlights over the audience at the arena. I gave him a few joints a few years ago, he caught up with me after today's rehearsal and gave me these."

He produced two joints, handing them to Chase.

"I'm going to need to know this guy's name," Chase told him.

"But if there's nothing wrong with these—"

"Look, laws about pot have changed. Possessing a couple of joints is nothing. Let me find out what the story is with this. First off, you no longer possess it, I do. And as for anyone else…at tops, small amounts are a fine and a few days in jail. But I'm not after you or anyone else just smoking a joint—we need the source."

Brandon nodded seriously. "Don't worry. Nothing for me in the next days except for a beer—in a bottle that's sealed when I get it!"

"Good thinking. Okay, I'll get this somewhere. I promise. And I'll let you know what's up in the morning. And if there is something in this…"

"I know, I know, I know. I got it from a guy named Bobby Sacks. He works lights."

"Thanks. Let's keep Bobby alive, okay?" Chase said.

"Thanks," Brandon told him. "Okay, uh, see you love-birds tomorrow, huh?"

"Yep, good night."

Brandon walked away. Knowing Sky was watching him, Chase still knew he had no choice.

"Just a sec," he told her, dialing Wellington's number. "Hey, um, a friend of mine got panicked when he saw the news. I have a couple of joints…um, yeah. I'll give you an address. You can pick them up from me there? I mean, I know you're a lecturer, but with what's going on… Great. I thought you might know what to do."

He hung up. "A friend who knows everyone in every lab from here to the ocean."

"Chase, my God, do you think—"

"I don't think anything right now. Let's let my friend get these to a lab, huh?"

She nodded and crawled into the car. They were silent on the way to the house. When they arrived, Larry was overjoyed to see them.

Sky might have said she didn't want a dog. But Larry evidently loved her.

And she loved Larry, it seemed.

"He's been sleeping on the couch, you know. And there are guest bedrooms here—"

"I guarantee you, when you go to bed, Larry will park himself in front of your door," Chase told her dryly. "I have to wait for my friend."

"I'll wait with you."

Before long, there was a buzz at the door. Chase looked

out— Wellington had come straight to Sky's house when he had called him.

"That's him?" Sky asked.

He nodded, hitting the release for the gate and the door. A minute later, he opened it to meet Wellington on the porch.

"Don't be rude—invite him in," Skylar said.

Larry woofed; she set a hand on his head, telling him that it was all right.

Chase had no choice. He stepped aside as he greeted Andy Wellington and introduced him to Sky as one of his lecturers.

"Sky Ferguson, what a pleasure!" Andy told her.

"And so nice to meet you, too. Brandon is a dear friend of ours, and we're so grateful he came to Chase and that Chase…knows people. Can we get you anything?" Sky said pleasantly.

"No, it's late, I'm just going to get these joints to friends I've met along the way," Wellington said politely. "But… Chase scored me some tickets for tomorrow night. I can't wait—you mostly disappeared, Miss Ferguson, and like me, tons of people out there are anxious to see you step into your father's shoes."

She shook her head. "I can't step into his shoes. I can only hope to honor him."

"I'm sure you will. He had an excellent reputation, and Chase tells me that all the amazing things written about him being an incredible human being are true."

Sky smiled and nodded. Wellington asked if he could pet the dog, and Sky assured him it was fine because he'd been identified as a friend.

Andy's eyes locked with Chase's for just a moment, and then he was gone.

"We'd really best get some sleep," Chase said.

"What did you think about Brandon? And...do you know this guy he was talking about? Bobby, who works lights?"

"I don't know Bobby. But—"

"Chase, if this stuff is laced, more people could die!"

"Wellington will get back to us as soon as possible and..." he shrugged "... I already told him Brandon got the stuff from Bobby Sacks."

She arched a brow at him.

"A little note I passed to him along with the joints."

She stared at him suspiciously. "Hey, let it get to the right people! If it was no big deal, it was no big deal. Well, hopefully, some lives will be saved."

"Shower," she said.

"Pardon?"

"There are three guest rooms upstairs and two more bathrooms. I'm for a shower and bed. Sleep wherever you like. I mean, we do have a dog now—one that your *friend* very specifically picked out for me. I'm going to assume he's an exceptional guard dog. Good night."

She turned and disappeared up the stairs. He watched her go and winced. There were moments when...

Time. Time could have gone away. He'd be holding her, just as he had those many years ago, he'd almost feel the softness of her flesh, the look in her eyes when...

First things first.

Keep them all alive.

Hell, they did have a big dog. He'd take a shower. And

his firearm would be on the sink, right next to the shower. No chances could be taken now.

A SHOWER FELT GOOD. Delicious. Hot water, and then, as it sluiced over her and she felt the steam and replayed the day in her mind, the day, and Chase…

Cold water.

Didn't help a lot.

He was there. There in her house. Close. She was standing in the shower, naked. He was probably in a shower, too…

Maybe. Maybe not. He seemed…

Well, he was paranoid about her, but with all his so-called friends, she couldn't tell what was really going on with him.

What the hell was he really doing for a living? He did love his grandfather, he'd always seemed to care about everyone involved with Skyhawk…

Impatiently, she turned off the water, stepped out and dried off, wrapping the towel securely around her. She stepped from her bathroom into the bedroom area, opened the door to the hallway cautiously and looked out.

Larry had indeed taken up a position right outside her door.

One room down, the door was closed.

She smiled. With Larry in the house, it seemed Chase had chosen to make use of an actual bed. As she stood there, she heard the faint sound of water going off.

Chase had opted for a shower and a bed.

She petted Larry's head, closed the door and headed for her dresser, seeking one of the oversize soft cotton T-shirts she liked to sleep in.

And then she had no idea of what really happened next. The show was coming up tomorrow—or later today, since it was after midnight.

Life…

Life was so fragile.

And at this moment her mind was, too.

And people in one's life were unique and rare, and she knew that and she'd never understood herself why she'd had to learn to live with loss on her own, why she hadn't clung to others who had cared.

She didn't know what she was thinking. No, she *wasn't* thinking. But she found herself stepping back out into the hall, heading to the door to the guest room that was closed, and opening it.

Chase was there, wrapped in a towel as she was, sorting through the clothing he had discarded but stopping dead as he saw her there.

"Sky?"

She shook her head. "Shut up. Please, just shut up."

She walked over to him, putting her arms around him, and drawing him into a deep, long kiss. And as she had hoped, prayed and maybe imagined, he pulled her closer to him, his arms wrapping around her, both towels slipping and falling away, and then their flesh, flesh touching, flesh, melding…

Time. Gone. An amazing burst of diamond and crystal light, the world exploding around them as they fell together onto the bed.

Touch came so easily, sweet, soaring sensuality as kisses roamed intimately between them, as the need and urgency grew, and they were together again…

Soaring, sweet ecstasy, excitement and the comfort of…
Love and security that had always been there, waiting.
As if they'd never been apart.

Chapter Six

"Why? Why did you push me away? Right when I might have helped you the most?" Chase whispered.

Sky looked at him, eyes a little desperate and, he thought, gave him the only answer she had.

"I don't know. I don't know! I was just..."

"Please tell me you know that I'd never have hurt your father," he said, his eyes on hers, searching, seeking.

"Maybe you'll never really be ready to forgive me!" she whispered.

He moved his fingers gently through her hair and then cupped her chin as he told her, "The past is gone, it is history, and we can't change history. But I loved you then, Skylar. I never stopped loving you, and I love you now."

She let out a soft cry, clinging closer to him, parting her lips as his mouth met hers in a passionate kiss that seemed a true promise of the words he'd spoken.

And later, they lay together, and he told her again that he'd always loved her and always would.

She smiled.

"Hey, that was an amazing declaration of my feelings, heart on my sleeve," he told her. "A response would be great."

She rolled over on an elbow to look down at him.

"Well, you know, you said it would be best if we pretended... I use all kinds of acting and improv techniques when I work with my students. When I'm doing something, well, you know, I try to do it right!"

He laughed, and she fell next to him again, whispering that she'd never understood, that maybe her pain had needed a different pain to twist her from her feelings. "I'll never understand myself, much less be able to explain myself!" she whispered.

"And it doesn't matter. What does matter is that we get some sleep," he said, wincing at the thought of the day to come.

She nodded, curling closer against him.

He closed his eyes, smiling. Amazing. If they could get past tomorrow...

He couldn't believe that they were together, that this... had happened. And for the moment, he was just going to hold her close.

SKY SLEPT AMAZINGLY WELL. She woke because light was coming through the windows, and she actually felt a chill.

She shouldn't have been cold with him next to her. But he wasn't there.

She must have slept incredibly deeply; he had gotten up and dressed and she hadn't heard a thing.

"Chase?" She said his name softly and sitting up, she was startled to see that there was a note taped to the inside of the door.

Frowning as she rose, she collected the note. She knew his handwriting.

Please don't freak out. I had to leave for a few minutes.

Couldn't leave you alone. Andy Wellington is downstairs with Larry. I asked him to watch over you.

Her frown deepened, but she quickly hit the lock on the bedroom door. Andy Wellington might be a friend and some kind of a law-enforcement lecturer, but she didn't know him. And this was her house! Chase shouldn't have...

Whatever!

She quickly gathered clothing and headed into the shower, anxious to bathe and dress as quickly as possible, reminding herself she was going to have to come back upstairs to choose an outfit for the show. She had a little rhinestone-studded tunic, and she thought she'd wear that over black jeans...kind of feminine, but pants to go with the guys.

Neither here nor there at the moment.

There was a stranger in her house!

She hurried on downstairs and found that Andy Wellington was indeed in the living room, seated on the couch with Larry curled at his feet. He had either a small tablet or a large phone, and he was engrossed in studying something that was on it.

He quickly looked up and rose as she entered the room.

"I'm so sorry. I don't mean to be intrusive, but we really didn't want you to be alone—even with Larry here."

She frowned, looking at him. "I really don't understand. I mean, you're a friend of Chase's, and that makes you welcome in my home, but..."

He looked down and when he looked up, his expression was acutely uncomfortable.

"I know that Chase is concerned, and other than that..."

She wasn't going to pick a fight with a stranger. She

lifted a hand and said, "Not to worry, I'll speak with Chase. Would you like coffee or anything?"

He shrugged. "I took the liberty. There's a pot made in the kitchen."

"Great. Thank you." She headed into the kitchen, followed by Larry, who was wagging his tail wildly.

Whatever else came of all this, she did love the dog. She checked his water and food bowls and realized that Chase had already seen to them.

"Well, Larry," she mused, "did you get to go out yet? Want to run around the yard?"

She walked back out. Andy Wellington was studying his device again with a frown on his face. She opened the door to let Larry run out joyfully into the yard. Then she approached Wellington.

"Is everything all right? Oh! By the way—the stuff that Brandon had last night, was it…tainted?"

He hesitated and then nodded. "Not to the point of instant death, but yes, it was contaminated."

"Oh, what about the guy that he got it from? Is he…?"

"Dead? No. I'm not sure what's going on exactly. We reported it to the right people immediately."

She nodded. "More friends of Chase's?"

"Friends of mine," he said. He shrugged. "I held a position in law enforcement for years. I know the right people."

"Ah. Well, I'm hoping he gets back soon."

"Me, too!"

"Don't let me interrupt your work," Sky told him. "I'm going to head to my office and go over the set list for tonight."

"Great. I'm here if you need me," he said. "Hey, can I get your phone number, please? I should have gotten it from Chase. I mean, well, seriously, there is bad stuff going on, and we should have each other's numbers."

She handed him her phone. "Grab my number and call me, and I'll have yours."

"Perfect, thanks."

She waited for him to get his number and call her. Then she took her phone back.

She smiled. "Just let Larry back in when he scratches at the door—which I believe he will in a few minutes."

"You got it."

She headed to her office thinking that she was going to have a hell of a lot to say to Chase when she saw him. She wasn't going to take it out on Wellington. The man was doing a friend a favor. It wasn't his fault that Chase had neglected to talk it all over with her.

Last night had been so good. So amazing…

And now? Now she realized that time had passed, and that there was so much she really didn't know about the man at all.

And yet…

There were still things she knew in her heart. He might annoy her—even anger her—but he was a good man. Trying his best, worried about her.

Still…

He had some answering to do!

THERE WAS ONE chance with the kind of overdose Bobby Sacks seemed to have suffered; luckily, it was something Chase had been trained to deal with and was prepared to administer: naloxone. He shot the dose into Bobby and began CPR.

He waited anxiously as Bobby's wife, tears in her eyes, looked on.

Then…

A gasp. Bobby inhaled. And by then the paramedics had arrived, and Chase could tell them what had happened and what he had done.

"That is one lucky man! I don't know if we'd have made it in time," one of the medics told him as Bobby was lifted onto a gurney and rolled out to the ambulance.

Chase shrugged. "I had a great mentor," he said. "Have you been called out on more of these?"

"So far, from what I've heard, anyone else afflicted has made it into the hospital," the medic told him. "Thankfully, people saw the news, and they're smart enough to get in—or throw away whatever the hell they bought. Carefully, I hope."

"Me, too," Chase murmured. "You'll be met at the hospital. When I called in, I was assured that this was something the FBI was on, so…"

"Got it. They'll be waiting until he can talk."

"I'll check on him later," Chase said.

The medic nodded; there would be police officers at the house, too, but he was grateful that Nancy Sacks, Bobby's wife, had called him. Apparently, she hadn't wanted Bobby arrested, but she'd been afraid of his behavior.

"Cops are coming?" she asked Chase when the paramedics were gone. "Bobby is going to live, right?"

"I believe so—we got him past the first hurdle in time. But I'm not a doctor—"

"But you did know what to do."

Nancy Sacks was an attractive woman with long brown hair and enormous hazel eyes. Chase had planned on paying Bobby Sacks a visit; he just hadn't expected to find him as he had.

Bobby had given the stuff to Brandon. But if he had been the one dealing it, he'd have known better than to indulge in his own product.

"All right, Nancy, from what I've heard, this has happened before—and it's the federal government that's following the trail. Someone will be here, yes. I take it you didn't join him for his little bit of recreation?"

"I hate pot—just makes me fall asleep," Nancy said. "But I never cared if Bobby had a puff here and there. I've known some drunks, and they're feisty and get into fist brawls. I've never seen a few puffers get dangerous toward anything other than a pile of food."

"Nancy, this is so important. Where did he get the stuff?"

She shook her head. "I don't know. From someone last night, I imagine, but I have no idea who. I mean, you know, he works those lights all the time for whatever is going on, and yeah, most of the time, things are available from someone. They kind of work on a trust arrangement, I guess. I don't know! Oh, Chase, I wish I knew. I mean... I knew how close you were to Jake Ferguson and I figured you learned a lot from him, but... Yeah, I guess we've all heard you're in some kind of a forensic school, so... I didn't know how bad it was going to get, I just called you—forgive me—because I didn't know I was going to need an ambulance... But, oh, my God, thank you! Bobby isn't a bad guy, he's good, he just..."

"Nancy, it's okay. But someone will be here and they'll want a statement. Or if you like, I can bring you to the hospital, and you can be there with Bobby and people will talk to you both while you're there."

"Please," she said.

He nodded and put a call through to Andy Wellington, telling him that he'd be back as soon as he'd dropped Nancy off.

"Well, that will be good," Wellington murmured.

Chase winced inwardly. He hadn't been sure how he was going to explain this one. And he didn't know why.

Gut fear, maybe because of everything going on.

But even with Larry in the house, he hadn't wanted Sky to be alone.

A dog could be shot. Then again, so could a man. But it was unlikely that a man like Wellington, who had spent his life in the service of the government after a stint in the military, was going to be taken by surprise.

Unlike Larry, he could shoot back.

"Let's get to the hospital," he told Nancy.

He hoped that Bobby might be conscious, but he doubted it. He believed that the man might make it.

But it would be a while before he could talk.

Chase just hoped it would be before the show that night.

SKY LIKED ANDY WELLINGTON well enough. There seemed to be little to dislike about him. He was polite and courteous, pleasant in every way.

She just didn't know what he was doing in her house. So, Chase had taken all kinds of classes. He knew all about so many things.

And they were both convinced her father had been murdered.

But what was he really doing?

She had left her office to make sure that Wellington was doing all right, still just seated on her sofa, when she heard the buzz that warned her someone was at the gate.

Larry woofed excitedly, wagging his tail.

That meant that Chase was back.

She hit the button that allowed the gate and door to open, and then she waited for him to come in. Naturally, he saw her staring at him the minute he walked in. And he knew she was going to want answers.

"Hey! Sorry, I had to run out. But under the current circumstances, I wanted someone to be with you and thankfully, you'd met Andy and you know—"

"Yeah. He carries a gun," Sky said, arms crossed over her chest.

Chase shrugged. "Yeah, I know you're safe with him."

Andy sat there silently, shaking his head, looking at Chase.

"I thought I was safe once I had a big dog," Sky said.

Andy spoke at last. "I didn't mean to be intrusive—" he repeated.

"You weren't," Sky quickly informed. "You're a perfect gentleman, welcome anytime. That's not the point."

They both just stared at her.

And then at one another.

"Just what the hell is going on here?" she demanded.

"I suggest you just tell her," Andy said quietly.

"Please! I suggest you just tell me, too," Sky said, staring hard at Chase. He couldn't mean her harm; even angry as she was, she couldn't doubt the feelings that enveloped them, as real as anything had ever been in her life.

But…

"Andy isn't just my friend. He's my SAC," Chase said.

"Sack?" Sky asked, confused.

"No, *SAC*, Special Agent in Charge," Chase explained.

"Um…in charge of what?" she asked.

Andy walked toward them both. "It's imperative that you keep this quiet. Special Agent Chase McCoy has been with the bureau for over two years, and he's an invaluable player in his undercover operations."

Sky shook her head, completely confused. "Undercover? Everyone knows who you are—well, anyone who is into rock bands and that kind of thing."

"Exactly," Andy Wellington explained.

Chase looked at Sky. "I'm sorry," he whispered.

"Well, yeah, you pretend well," she said. "But I still—you mean, none of this is because of my father, you're really working for…the government?"

"Yes and no. I really work for the government, but no one knows except my folks and Hank. And as to your dad? I work for the government because of him," Chase said flatly.

Sky stared at him, frowning. Chase explained, "I never believed it. I never believed that Jake Ferguson would inadvertently rip up an amp when a wire had come loose. I—I believed he saw something that night, and whatever he saw caused someone to make sure he never got a chance to tell anyone else."

She shook her head. "I don't understand—"

"No one knows, Sky. I told you. No one knows but Wellington, some fellow agents, my parents, and Hank. And now you. Because it's imperative for the kind of work I do that everyone thinks I am what I am in the other half of my life, the grandson of Hank McCoy, drummer and vocalist for the rock band Skyhawk."

She was silent, not sure what to think or feel.

"Why didn't you tell me?" she asked.

He didn't reply.

"Be fair, Sky," Wellington said quietly. "He hadn't seen you in years."

"But…"

She just shook her head and turned away.

"Sky," Chase said.

"Let me deal!" she snapped.

And apparently, her state of mind wasn't the most important thing at the moment, because Wellington was quickly speaking with Chase.

"Bobby. You got to him in time."

Chase nodded. "I don't know what's out there, if it's the same source… The stuff Brandon had was contaminated, but not badly enough to kill. This stuff that Bobby had… was bad. And the thing is, Bobby can't be the dealer—small stuff, giving to friends or whatever. He has a great wife, good work—I don't really know him, but from what I've seen when I have been around the venue, he's a solid worker and loves his wife and family and has no desire to die."

"You know him enough—his wife called you," Wellington said.

"And I think it was the right call for me to get there," Chase said quietly.

"Yeah. You've done this—had the equipment and the knowledge to do what was needed. Let's hope he makes it. And that he comes around…in time."

"We have no idea how much is out there," Chase said.

Sky was watching and listening in astonishment. She thought she knew Chase. Even after years away. She'd asked about him casually. She'd looked him up online. It always seemed that he'd been playing or taking classes or...

Maybe she actually knew Chase better than she'd imagined. This was, on the one hand, all a shock. On the other hand...

It wasn't surprising Chase would be an agent, that a young man who had listened to and admired her father had learned to save lives...

And to fight the bad guys.

"All right. We know Brandon had stuff—and Bobby had it. We need to find the main snake and cut its damned head off," Wellington said. "This has gone on too long."

"My grandfather and Bobby are at the same hospital. I thought I'd take a minute to visit Hank, and then I can check on Bobby as well. NOPD is on it—guards are in the hall," Chase said. "Sir, if you could be with Sky a bit longer—"

"No, no, no, no, no," Sky said flatly.

They both stared at her.

"Now that I know what the hell is going on, Chase, I'm sticking with you. I haven't seen Hank, and I'd very much like to. You just said NOPD is at the hospital, too. I'm going with you." She turned to Wellington. "Thank you, Mr. SAC, sir. I appreciate everyone worrying about how I get to keep on living. But I will be fine now with Chase, and I'd very much like to see Hank."

Chase and Wellington stared at one another for a moment.

She had a feeling Wellington was silently assuring Chase it was his call.

"All right. So Larry guards the house, and we all head out," Chase said.

"And you'll be at the venue by four?" Wellington asked Chase.

Chase nodded. "Last tech."

"I'll be there, an old lecturer, in awe of a classic-rock band," Wellington said.

Chase nodded. "And we may find nothing, despite all our determination."

"Something is going on. And we will find the truth," Wellington said. "Well, I'll leave you for now. Give Hank my regards. I'll just say goodbye to Larry and be out of here."

"Thank you, sir," Sky told him.

He smiled at her. She did like the man. And if Chase was working directly beneath him, it was good to know him.

When he was gone, Chase watched her in silence.

"So nothing about you is real."

He shook his head. "Sky, everything about me is real. And that's why…it's why what I do works."

"Hey, you were honest at first. You said we needed to pretend."

"Sky, nothing with you is pretend!" he vowed.

She nodded. "Well, we'll see. Busy afternoon—let's get to the hospital."

"I'll see to Larry—"

"I have food and water set out for him already," Sky said. The dog was next to her, her constant companion—and guard.

Well, if all else went astray, she'd gotten a great dog out of it all.

She petted Larry's head and told him to guard the house and started out, leaving Chase to follow her and check on the locks to the house and the gate as they left.

His car was there, ready, on the street right in front of her house.

She was silent as they drove. So was he.

But when they reached the hospital, he turned to her at last. “Sky, please. I swear this is true—what happened with your dad set me on this path. But it’s incredibly important that no one else knows.”

“Did you think I was going to announce it on stage tonight?” she asked him. She knew her tone was sharp and sarcastic, but she had trusted him. And she had thought that he trusted her.

Even if they’d been apart.

He didn’t respond. They exited the car and headed up into the hospital, pausing for their visitor credentials at the desk.

Sky followed him as they walked straight to Hank’s room.

Hank was in a chair by the bed, watching the news. Sky was glad to see he looked good: his color was healthy, and he smiled broadly as he saw her coming in behind Chase.

“Sky!” he said with pleasure.

She smiled and hurried to him, bending to give him a hug and a kiss on the cheek.

“Sweetie, it’s wonderful to see you,” he told her.

“You, too, Hank. And you look—”

“Thanks! I get out of here in a few days. I think they’re being overly cautious, but, hey…my grandson is a dictator. And I will do everything they tell me. I’m anxious to come back to the drums myself. Oh, and if you’re going to start playing with those guys often, I have a great gift for you. Seriously, half the drummers I know are deaf now! But I found these great earplugs—they let you hear, but they keep out the deafening volume. These are just about perfect!"

"Thanks, Hank. I'm sure Chase appreciates them," Sky said sweetly.

"There are tons of perks to what we do," Hank said. "And a few drawbacks, but there's a set of the earplugs in my drawer. I'd love you to have them." He grinned. "There's no way I get to play this gig, so please take them?"

"Take them or he'll make me crazy," Chase said.

"Hey! You have hearing thanks to me!" Hank said.

Chase grinned at him. "And I can play the drums, too, thanks to you. No lack of appreciation meant, just—"

"He's a dictator!" Hank assured Sky, grimacing, and shaking his head. "But other than that, a good enough kid. So how are you? Ran into a friend of yours before I found myself in here, Sky. Virginia Hough. She said you were a miracle worker with troubled kids, that they spent time with you, got deep into music and showmanship and stopped being so much trouble."

"Virginia is a lovely woman," Sky said, shrugging. "I like kids. I like working with them. One of the students I had the first year I was working went on to become great at improv—he's working at an improv comedy club in South Florida. It's great, Hank. Really rewarding."

"Like the boy here," Hank murmured. He looked quickly at Chase. "Always trying to learn something new!" he added.

"It's all right, Hank. She knows," Chase said. As he spoke, he frowned suddenly. She saw he was looking out the small window of the door to Hank's room. "Excuse me," he said. "I'll be right back."

He left the room. Sky watched him go, lowering her head and smiling slightly.

The place was crawling with police. That would be the only reason he'd be away from her, she knew.

"Kid he saved is down the hall," Hank said quietly.

"I heard…something," Sky said.

"I am proud of him. Chase was in a place where he could have gone on to be the top of top—but he went on to do something he saw as being more important."

"And he knew what to do for…for what happened," Sky said.

"He still takes classes all the time. He's like a sponge, wants to know everything and it all makes him invaluable. And…" Hank looked down, a frown tearing into his forehead.

Hank, as a grandfather, was still an impressive man. Even in a hospital chair, he had a strong face, solid jaw, bright eyes and his headful of handsome white hair.

She imagined that one day, Chase would look like him. Or maybe Chase did look like a young Hank, as he must have looked all those years ago when Skyhawk had first hit the scene.

"He never believed what happened to my father was an accident," Sky said.

Hank looked up at her. "Neither did I," he told her. He shook his head. "Your dad and I… You know, I was the one with the garage. My folks let me have a drum set out there. And your dad started coming over, and the two of us were the beginning of it all. He just…he just had it! I'd heard the story that his dad wanted him drafted, that he wouldn't do anything about getting him into college to get out of Vietnam. I thought it was the cruelest thing I'd ever heard. But Jake told me, no, that it was the best thing in the world for him. His dad had told him that if he was going to kill himself, at least he could do it for his country."

"I heard," Sky said softly.

"He said war was brutal. And it hurt him—he lost friends he made in the service. But for him, it turned out to be a lifesaver. He'd been given back a chance in a double way, and he was going to be smart and grateful for all his years to come. I loved him, Sky."

"I know you did, Hank. He loved you, too."

"He made us all better musicians—and better human beings."

Sky smiled, hunkered down by his side and took his hands. "Thank you, Hank. I know that after what happened… I was horrible for a while. Now…"

"Now you want the truth. And I understand. So does Chase. And I believe in him, Sky. I believe in my grandson. If something can be done, Chase will be the one to see that it is."

"Where do you think he's gotten off to?" Sky asked.

Hank shrugged. "Well, he knows the place is swimming with cops, and you're safe in here with me. That kid he saved—I say *kid* loosely at my age—anyway, like I said earlier, he's just down the hall. Maybe he's conscious."

"And Chase is trying to find out what he can from him?"

"I would think. So tell me about tonight. Are you at all excited? Did you really want to perform? Are you doing it just to try to discover what happened in the past?"

"Both. If I can honor my dad, I'm glad to do so. If I can find the truth, so much the better. I should have said if *we* can find the truth. I didn't realize until we got into this in the last couple of days just how ill-equipped I was to find out anything."

Hank smiled. "You're in good hands, I promise. Even if…"

"If?"

Hank shrugged. "I read people."

"Oh?"

"Well, hmm. You care about Chase. You two were like a pair of lovebirds back then, and I got the feeling…well, the feeling is there. But you're not sure you trust him."

"Okay, truthfully? I just found out he was working for the government."

"He's not at liberty to share that, you know."

"*You* know," she said softly.

He nodded. "I know. Being him… Okay, he is my grandson. But he's also an amazing human being, Sky. Then again, so are you. You're both the family of rock royalty, and yet you see the world in a bigger way. And that's great. But don't forget one thing."

"What's that?"

"Your dad invented and loved Skyhawk. The rest of us… Well, he was the one who found out how we could make and record our music, he was our main songwriter. He loved the band, and he loved telling stories with his songs. Remember that. You're truly honoring him when you get up there on that stage and channel him and all that he loved."

"Thanks, Hank."

He nodded. "And trust Chase. It's not his fault he can't tell anyone."

"I'm not just *anyone*. He knew what I was doing right

away, and right away he wanted to help me. But he didn't trust me."

"Forgive him. He has his reasons for keeping his life a total secret."

"Right, but…it was *me*."

"And I'm sure he was in torture over not being able to say anything. In fact—"

He broke off. His door suddenly burst open. A man entered, leaned against the door to shut it, and looked out through the window. While carefully studying the hall, he pulled out a gun.

Chapter Seven

Bobby Sacks was awake and aware, but just barely.

Chase should have felt relief, grateful when he spoke with the man's doctor and was told that his arrival and quick action had saved Bobby's life.

The doctor himself had been the one to summon Chase; there was an officer from NOPD just outside his door. Another officer had just gone downstairs with Bobby's wife so she could take a break and get something to eat in the cafeteria.

"Also figured you might want a minute—just a minute, he's not very strong—to speak with him alone," the doctor had said.

Chase had appreciated his help: naturally, it was imperative to save a life first. And sometimes, law enforcement really had to wait to question a suspect or a witness.

This man had seen to it that he'd get a few minutes immediately.

Bobby opened his eyes as the doctor left and Chase stood by his bed. He winced and tried to smile. "You're supposed to be a drummer. My wife said you're known for taking forensics classes and that...you saved my life when she didn't know what to do. Thank you."

"I'm glad you're alive," Chase assured him. "But, Bobby—"

"Yeah, I know. I saw a guy briefly when I wasn't really…well, aware enough to say much. I know. I don't want others to die."

"But you gave Brandon some weed."

"Different lots."

"Where did you get your drops of the drugs? Different drops?"

"I…I don't know."

"How can you not know?"

"I leave the money wherever I'm told to leave it. Then I get a message back. I…well, I meant to be generous with friends. I made a buy twice."

"How do you make the buy?" Chase asked.

"The web." He hesitated. "The dark web."

"So you make arrangements online—on the dark web—and someone tells you where to leave money and then where to pick up the stash?"

Bobby Sacks winced as he nodded. "I never thought… I mean, I'd heard about drugs that were laced, but I never thought… It's been a long time… When Skyhawk is playing…" He shrugged weakly. "Maybe some other times. I don't… I don't know. I guess that sometimes when other groups or acts are performing…"

"I'm glad you're going to be okay, Bobby, really. Thing is, what happened to you could happen to someone else. I mean, I'm not up on the dark web, but I'll let the cops or whoever know, and they'll get someone to you with a computer, and you can help them find the source of whatever is going on here. I've got to do that."

"I know!" he said, wincing. "Chase, believe me, I don't

want anyone dying! I don't want anyone hurt or dying because of me!"

"Right. I'll—"

A male nurse was coming into the room, carrying a tray with a shot of medicine to be added to Bobby's IV.

"Hey," he said, greeting them both. "Doc just ordered this for you. It will take me two seconds. Oh, I've been asked to tell your visitor he's been here long enough. You need to get some rest."

Chase glanced at the needle. There seemed to be something off. It should have been an ordinary procedure; he'd seen the staff add medications to his grandfather's IV often enough.

But something looked different. The man was dressed in the same scrubs as the other nurses, but something didn't seem right.

"What is that?" Chase asked him.

"Oh, uh, just a little more saline, get him better hydrated," the nurse said.

He looked to be a man in his late thirties or early forties. And if he was a nurse, he shouldn't have suggested that a shot so small was but saline.

"You're not putting that in his arm," Chase said.

"What? I just told you—"

"No. Step away from him," Chase said.

He saw the man reach behind his back and knew that he was reaching for a weapon. He could have pulled his own. Instead, he made a flying leap, bringing the man down to the floor before he could draw his gun.

The weapon went flying across the floor.

The ostensible nurse went for it, stretching to retrieve it.

Chase caught him by the ankle, shouting for one of the cops.

In two seconds, NOPD's finest were in the room with him. He explained quickly that the man had tried to put something in Bobby's IV then gone to draw his weapon. He needed to give this one to the cops; he didn't want to have to show the credentials he kept but never used.

The officers quickly had the guy cuffed and up. He stared at Chase with loathing and then started to laugh. "Hotshot drummer. Think you're tough 'cause you got the money for hours at the gym, huh? You'll get yours—trust me. You'll get yours!"

"We've got him, Mr. McCoy. We've got him," one of the cops assured him.

"Thanks!" Chase said.

They dragged the suspect out of the room, aggravated that they hadn't seen that something was wrong when he'd gone in.

Chase made a mental note to tell Wellington they needed someone in the hospital who knew something about medicine—either that or make sure nothing went into Bobby's IV unless the doctor himself administered it.

"Man, wow, you are…well, one hell of a drummer," Bobby said, looked at him in despair and shaking his head. "You did it again—you saved my life again. How the hell…"

"I knew that wasn't saline. I've had my share of family in the hospital," Chase said, shrugging. "And what the hell, I haven't even done any drumming here. Listen, I'm going to see to it that the people who matter know what happened and make sure you're safe. I'll take care of that right now. Your wife will be back up in a minute, and they'll let her stay—but I'm going to see to it that someone who knows what's up is here, too. At all times."

"Man, thank you. Thank you, thank you!" he said softly.

Chase nodded, heading for Bobby's door. As he set his hand on it, he heard a sound that could only be that of a shot, explosive, painfully loud in the peace and quiet of the hospital floor.

SKY DIDN'T MEAN to scream; the sound of the shot was so startling, so loud, she let out a gasp that was part squeak and part scream.

"It's all right, it's all right!" the man in Hank's room quickly informed them. "I'm Luke Watson, NOPD. There's—I don't know what—but you're safe, my job is to stand right here and shoot anyone who tries to come near either of you," he assured them.

Sky swallowed hard and said the only thing that came to mind.

"Thank you, thank you. But Chase—"

"Chase will be fine. There are cops all over this place. Whatever is going on, we all have our assignments, and you are mine," Watson said.

Sky nodded, hoping against hope he was for real, because he wasn't wearing a uniform.

As if he could sense her thoughts, the man turned, still keeping his peripheral vision on the door but reaching into his pocket.

Not for a gun, she prayed.

His credentials.

"Thank you," she whispered again, gripping Hank's hand tightly.

She had wanted to find the truth. Now, she was sure

she knew it. Her father *had* seen something, known something, and he had died for it.

Just as someone was apparently trying to kill others now.

Fear seemed to grip her like chilled and bony fingers around the heart.

She needed to know. She needed to know so badly. And yet…she had never imagined this kind of danger, a killer slipping into a hospital, shots fired *in a hospital*!

She thought about being on stage that night but remembered there would be security stations and security guards. Bags would be checked and arrivals would go through metal detectors.

What had happened with Jake had been far more subtle.

Whoever was doing this didn't want to get caught. But then…

The man drew the door open, letting Chase enter. He was anxious and tense, asking quickly, "You're all right? Everything is all right?"

"We're good. Officer Watson here is great," Hank assured him quickly.

Chase stared at Watson and gave him a nod of thanks.

Then Chase was gone again.

"Where… He needs to be here!" Sky whispered.

"Trust him!" Hank whispered.

"Trust is a two-way street!" she whispered in return. But she realized she was afraid.

Afraid for herself. And worse.

She was afraid for Chase.

"STAIRWELL!" ONE OF the uniformed cops in the hall shouted. "Headed down the stairwell!"

He was moving quickly, racing to the stairs.

Chase hurried behind him, drawing his weapon and assuring him, "I have a permit! I can help, I swear, I've worked with lots of cops, and I am not at all trigger-happy."

The cop nodded as they headed in the direction of the gunfire.

They almost tripped over one of the police officers who had just been in Bobby Sacks's room, one who had cuffed the fake nurse.

He groaned; the man was shot but still alive.

"LeBlanc!" the officer with Chase cried, hunkering down by the fallen man.

"Stay with him—get help!" Chase ordered, knowing he needed to move fast.

"He got Harvey's gun…he's got Harvey!" the man on the floor moaned.

"I'll get him!" Chase promised, hurrying down the stairs. He didn't hear the explosion of another shot. He did hear scuffling and then a whisper that was oddly echoed in the stairwell.

"Move, move, move…and you may live!"

Despite his speed, Chase forced himself to move as quietly as possible, finally seeing the nurse and the cop as he rounded one turn. He took aim at the nurse's head, shouting out, "Stop now! Lower the gun!"

Instead, the nurse laughed and took aim, pointing his weapon directly at him. But Chase was ready, sliding back to avoid the bullet that plowed into the wall while carefully returning fire.

The nurse didn't let out a peep.

Chase had caught him squarely in the forehead. He fell, rolling down the last few stairs to the first-floor landing.

Chase cursed himself as he hurried down to reach the officer—Harvey as the other man had called him. He was staring at Chase with gratitude.

"He was going to kill me. He shot my partner—he was just using me to get out of the hospital. He would have killed me. How..."

"I've worked with law enforcement and have the proper credentials to carry, and he was after people in this hospital. My grandfather is here," Chase said.

The cop looked at him. "You're one hell of an interesting drummer, Mr. McCoy."

"Um, yeah, I've heard that."

"Thank you. I need to see to my partner—"

"He was talking, and being in a hospital, he'll get immediate help."

"And...well, we'll need your weapon, and you'll have to make a statement. I mean, you saved my life, but the world runs on paperwork. Real paper, sometimes."

Chase nodded, looking at the dead suspect.

Was he the pusher? He'd never seen the man before.

"Well, I guess you have to call someone, but I'd like to get back to my grandfather," Chase said. "If that's okay. I'll be here... I am due at our tech rehearsal at four, but—"

To his relief, Chase saw that Wellington had arrived with the captain of the local PD.

"Mr. McCoy, the police need your weapon, and they'll be asking you to sign a statement. We need to do this quickly. Captain Hughes and I both have tickets for tonight's event—we can't have you missing anything and we don't want to miss anything, either!"

"I need to see my grandfather and Sky," Chase said.

"Of course. You are something, Mr. McCoy. Johnnyon-the-spot, and a big show tonight! Grateful you were here," Wellington said. "Come on, son, we'll head on back up, I'll get you onto the paperwork, and then we'll get you to the show!"

OF COURSE, Sky figured, Wellington had all kinds of strings he could pull. He left Hank's room again with Chase, but the two returned within a few minutes—paperwork all done.

Even for Wellington, that must have been quite a feat. But then, from what she began to understand, Chase had now saved the life of a cop as well, and that had to sit well with whoever pulled all the strings.

They finally bade Hank goodbye with Chase warning him to do everything the doctors told him to do—and Hank warning Chase to be careful.

"Always careful," Chase told him.

"I didn't see today as—"

"That's because you weren't looking. I am always careful," Chase assured him.

Hank's face—half smile and half frown—showed his pride in his grandson. Sky, of course, was grateful. Chase did seem to have a knack for getting the bad guys.

Her father had given him that determination.

Of course, she was proud, too. And still a little bit scared. She'd been angry that he hadn't trusted her. But inwardly, she could admit she now understood. He was undercover. Undercover…as himself. And all his classes had been real—apparently, he'd learned a great deal about drugs, drug overdoses and how to reverse them.

He also seemed to have instinct, something one probably couldn't get in any class, more likely something that was basic to certain people.

She was quiet as they headed to the last rehearsal before the concert.

She was surprised when Chase spoke, his voice pained. "I'm thinking we should cancel the show. Wellington even mentioned it to me."

"What?" she demanded.

He shook his head. "It's one thing for me to step into something that could turn very bad—I made that choice. But after the events at the hospital, I don't know what we're looking at."

"I put me in it—I'm choosing to do so."

"It's a concert. No one should die over a concert."

"People are dying without the concert. The concert is your way of finding out what is really going on, just how deep it all runs. Chase, I want to do it. Not just for…not just for one reason. I want to do it for my father. Hank reminded me of something today. My dad loved the band—he created it. He truly believed in that saying, that music could soothe the savage beast. And I've got it—someone is using Skyhawk events for something so bad it's pure evil. But this is the chance to stop it. To save lives. You got to do that today. Chase, I want my chance to be a part of something bigger, too."

He was silent.

"Wellington would understand. Oh, and Wellington will make sure the metal detectors are working overtime, and the audience is half cops and agents, probably, Louisiana State Police, you name it."

Again, he was silent.

"I'm right, aren't I?"

"You'll be center stage," he said quietly.

"You betcha!" she said determinedly. "Chase, people have seen on the news that drugs have been laced and contaminated, that people are dying. I don't think so many will be wanting to buy stuff. But I do think that whoever was doing what—the person my father knew was involved—is going to be there. And under these circumstances…"

"Yeah, he could slip up," Chase admitted. "Still—"

"I'm going to be all right. Chase, Charlie made a point—none of us touches equipment. If something is going to happen, it will be to one of them. Not that I want anything to happen, I don't mean it that way, but—"

"I don't think whoever from our group is involved is the kingpin—but if we can get someone who can talk—"

"Bobby didn't help any?"

"I think he will help. Wellington is getting a computer whiz in there with him." He hesitated and shrugged. "Bobby knows he almost died. And he has a great wife, a good job."

"So what did he tell you?"

"The dark web."

"It is real," she murmured.

"Very real."

"I mean, I knew that, I just…"

"We'll see," he said. They'd reached parking for the performers, and he turned to her again. "Sky, if anything was to happen to you—"

"And if anything was to happen to you," she interrupted.

He nodded slowly. She set her hands on his. "Okay, seriously, I know you think you're stronger, that some machismo is kicking in—"

"No. Honestly. Training. Sky, you know I've been to a million classes—"

"That won't stop a bullet."

"No. But I know how to watch and hit a fly at a hundred yards when I need to. But I don't think there are going to be firearms at the concert—"

"Then, you don't need to be worried that I'll be a target."

He was silent. She knew he really didn't think firearms were something they needed to concerned about.

But he was still worried.

"I'm not going to touch any equipment, Chase," she told him. "I'm just going to be there—drawing out whoever might be doing something, or not even drawing them out. I'll just be making sure the show goes on so they can do whatever it is they do."

He nodded. "Yep, right. Okay then, shall we?"

The exited the car and headed in. Chris Wiley and Brandon were there, checking mics and instruments with Justin, Nathan and Charlie.

Charlie, naturally, looked at them anxiously. Chase clapped him on the back, and Sky knew he was hoping Charlie would act normally.

She assumed, however, that Chase had gotten with him. He knew about Bobby Sacks. He would have made sure, too, that Charlie was all right.

And that he should keep quiet.

"Hey!" Chris called, greeting them. He hurried over and gave Chase a pat on the back and hugged Sky.

"This is going to be amazing! Sky, so cool," he said softly.

"Thanks. Of course."

"Mark has the set list. Sound checks..."

"Wait, wait!" Mark came hurrying in from the stage-right wing. "Sky, we've another reporter who wants to speak with you before we get started. Obviously, we want the best tech we can get, but I also know that you knew your dad, you'll play it by ear and audience cue once we get going—"

"Mark, yes, I'll be fine." She smiled and added sincerely, "I'm happy to be here. And I will be my dad to the very best of my ability."

Mark Reynolds smiled at her. "No, Sky. Honor your dad, but be you. This band, the group of us, we're his legacy in a way. But you're his real legacy. Be you!"

Joe Garcia had followed Mark in. "Be you, Sky," he echoed. But then he grimaced and added, "But you might tell the reporter you think we're ultracool."

Sky laughed. "Joe, I've got it. No worries," she assured him.

"Hey!"

She turned around. Charlie was attaching a wire to an amp.

"Hey, Charlie."

"You're all here. No one, and I mean no one but Nathan, Justin or me, is to touch anything electric or electronic, got it?" he demanded.

"You got it!" Mark assured him, glancing worriedly at Sky.

She set a hand on his arm. "It's okay." She turned, smiling. "Not to worry, Charlie. I won't even fool with my own fuse box!"

He looked at her and nodded. She smiled. He was definitely looking worried. She decided it was a good thing Chase was the one working undercover and not Charlie.

"I've got the reporter just back there. Her name is Marci Simmons. Seems nice and already told me she loves her job because she loves rock bands," Mark said.

"Great. I'll go talk to her." She turned and almost tripped over one of the workers she didn't know.

"Sorry, sorry!" he said. "I'm, uh, Noah. Noah Lawson. I'm kind of new. But I'm super happy to be here, and I didn't mean to be in your way!"

"No, no, it's fine!" she reassured him.

Smiling, she headed into the stage-right wing. A woman was waiting for her by the dressing rooms.

"Hi, I'm Marci!" she said, offering Sky a hand. "I realize you guys want to get to it, but I'd love to ask you a few questions. This is a really special occasion. Chase McCoy sitting in for Hank—and you, which is truly rare, taking your dad's place."

"I'm happy to be here," she said.

"Even though…"

"My father loved the band. He loved music. All forms of music. And he was from New Orleans, fell in love with street musicians, Frenchmen Street and all the venues. Dad loved his songs. I'm happy to do his songs."

"He was all about the music, right?"

"And people," Sky said. "He truly enjoyed other musicians. Oh, and musical theater! He told me he'd been crazy about *Godspell* and *Jesus Christ Superstar* when he'd been young. He loved *Tommy*, and then, coming up to closer decades, *Hamilton* and *Next to Normal*. He appreciated so many of his fellow performers."

"They say he admired others. Some rock stars want it to be all about them and don't really care to watch other—"

Sky interrupted her with an honest laugh. "Trust me! My dad wanted to go to just about any concert—he loved his old friends and acquaintances and new talent. And then again, any musical theater anywhere near him."

"His songs—"

"Tended to reflect his life."

"Well, here's an important question for you. We understand you use music to teach, often with those who are having difficulty with behavioral problems or fitting in—kids maybe even at risk. Will you keep doing that, or will you be with Skyhawk full-time now?"

"I love what I do. But I'm not saying I won't be with Skyhawk again. On the one hand, I was my father's baby. On the other hand, the band was equally his creation. I'd like to honor music in the way that he loved it and the band."

"That's great, and thank you so much!" the young woman said. "I am truly anxious to see the show and equally grateful for this chance to chat briefly with you."

"My pleasure," Sky assured her.

She left Marci, aware that activity was already happening on the stage, with sound and mic checks. They'd be ready for her.

She paused. Brandon was next to Chris, listening to all last-minute instructions from his father. Nathan was working on something with the keyboard. Joe and Mark were both strumming guitars, talking about chords. Charlie and Justin were working on something with an amplifier and the drums.

But she wasn't the only one who hadn't been on stage.

Chase wasn't there.

Frowning, she looked around and saw he was in the audience. He was engaged in conversation with an audience member.

Andy Wellington. She knew Chase: while it might appear the two men were having a casual conversation, she could tell he had just learned something. Something that brought a furrow to his brow. But Brandon approached the two of them, and Chase quickly smiled and introduced the two men.

"Sky?"

She spun around. Nathan was there. "Mic check?" he asked her.

"Um, yeah, sure, of course!" she replied.

She went through the motions. And she hoped she'd get a private minute with Chase again before they plowed straight into tech…

And the performance.

One that might be far more than anyone involved had begun to imagine.

"BOBBY HAS BEEN GREAT, amazing, really," Wellington told Chase. "Of course, we have some great people working for us who can crack almost anything ever done on or with a computer."

"They found the source?" Chase said.

Wellington nodded, smiling, as if they were speaking about songs or the weather. "The signal bounced all over, from here to Asia, Europe, Africa…South America, and back here. But in the end, the origin was right here, in Orleans Parish. Finding the actual physical place where the initial site was created is proving a bit difficult—personal computers move all over the place, and registrations can be as false as anything else. But someone here is being played by someone bigger. What I'm trying to figure is why? We've checked the financials on the band. You know yourself every member does well enough. No one is in this for the money, so..."

"But you think it is someone with the band."

"Someone close. The band or the roadies."

Chase had nodded, then lowered and shook his head.

Who? Why? None of them needed money.

"So," he said, "no one with a gambling problem, no one who lost big in cryptocurrency or anything of the sort?"

"We have truly had people all over this. I'm convinced they are working through one of the cartels. But again, *why* is a mystery. These guys don't need money."

Chase knew they didn't have much time for a private conversation. As others moved near them or passed by, he introduced Wellington, who behaved like the perfect—if slightly reserved—fan.

He glanced on stage, wishing that his heart didn't skip a beat as he watched Sky at the mic.

She wasn't touching it, she was standing back, singing a few bars, doing a sound check. They were testing just her mic, she was singing a cappella, and he was touched by the song she had chosen, her dad's ode to the beauty of life once one learned how to live it.

"The sun so bright, such a promise, beauty and light,
Yet those same lights can turn to night,
Darkness deep, with just a blaze, one that burns,
While it promises to amaze,
But the pain sets in, and there seems no hope,
Tangled there in a million ropes,
Just broken bits and pieces of me

Pieces longing again to see…
Find the freedom in true light,
Seek the stars in the darkness of night,
And finding the light is hard, so hard,
But it can be captured if you fight the fight,
And once again, you'll find true light,
Hold it loose and hold it dear,
and you'll discover that the light is near…"

There were choruses that came in, harmonies, and it was an amazing song, both beautiful and with a rock beat that had made it an instant success. But that day, listening to Sky, knowing what it had meant to her because of what it had meant to Jake, was beautiful.

Jake had found the true light. He'd battled hard, he'd tortured his parents and others who had loved him, but he'd proved himself in the end.

And then he'd died, determined that he would do what was right for others.

They were doing a sound check, just a sound check, and yet when Sky finished, there was silence in the room. Then applause.

Applause…

Except Chase noticed Justin. He wasn't applauding. He was staring at Sky. Staring at her…as if something inside of him was broken and burning as well.

He felt his phone buzz.

He glanced down.

Dark web encrypted but the source—here.

He closed his phone and looked at Justin again. He had to get the man alone.

Chapter Eight

Sky found herself chatting with Joe about the songs, and then Mark about their set lists. Chris joined them as well, telling her that the full rehearsal with her the night before had been like speeding back through the years to a beautiful time.

"You, Brandon, Chase…having you guys here is incredible," he told her, smiling. He grimaced. "You kind of, hmm…what are the words I'm looking for? Make everything perfect. We were good from the beginning—your dad made us good musicians, and he kept us all together as friends. I mean, a lot of the old groups are still playing, but most have new members in them somewhere. Folks like us, from the seventies and eighties…we lost a lot of amazing artists. Janis Joplin, Elvis, Michael Jackson, Prince, so very many…and then, hey, you get where we are and there are deaths from natural causes, too. But think of the groups and performers still out there—Bruce Springsteen, Elton John, Billy Joel—your dad loved all of them, said they were real songsters! 'Piano Man,' Billy Joel, one of his favorites. The Eagles! So many more. But with us…your dad is gone and Hank is recovering, but we have family members! True legacy."

"Thanks, Chris," she told him. "It's great fun to be with Brandon, too."

"Yep, the boy is coming along nicely. But…" He shrugged.

"What?" Sky asked him.

"Thing is, being us has been great. We made money, and your dad was the guy who led us. We were so young, but we never went crazy. He got us the right management and the right financial advisers. Thing is, as much as I've loved being Skyhawk, what I want to leave behind is hard to explain."

Brandon walked up, joining them. "You're not going anywhere for a long time!" he told his father sternly.

"Not planning to," Chris assured him, "but none of us ever really knows. I don't know how to express it, but I'm so glad, so damned glad, you three younger people are with us—but what I hope we leave behind is something that isn't performing in front of a crowd or getting a good paycheck. It can't really be touched. It's just the love of music, what music can do when you're down, how it can help bring you back up, how… Wow. I just sound weird—"

"Nothing new there!" Brandon teased.

"Hey! Careful, I'll ground you!" Chris teased in return. He ran his fingers through his hair and then paused. "Like this stuff on my head. It's white—"

"Ah, but still there! You still look like a great rocker!" Sky assured him.

He laughed softly. "Like I said, it's just darned great that there are a bunch of us still out there—some of them even make me feel young! Anyway, Sky, hope you'll join us now and then. Thing is—well, I know you love what you do. You take music someplace special and do special things with it when you work with kids, so… I hope you can keep doing what you love, and still throw some gigs in with us old-timers now and then, too."

She gave him a quick hug. "Chris, thank you, and I hope so, too."

Nathan called Chris, asking him to come check something on the keyboard. Chris hurried off, and Brandon grimaced at Sky.

"And here we all are."

"And you, sir, are great on the keyboards and backup. And you play lead guitar, too!"

Brandon laughed. "I try. Anyway, I'm happy to be here. We'll have fun."

She smiled. "Sure. Lots of fun!"

"The special friend group is arriving," Brandon said using air quotes and almost whispering as if someone might have heard them from the audience. "There's that guy Chase knows—some kind of a forensic expert, does all kinds of lecturing."

"Yeah, I met him. Andy Wellington. Nice guy," Sky assured him.

"Yeah, he seems okay. And there's Justin's wife, Julia," Brandon pointed out. "Wonder who that guy she's with is. She usually shows up with the kids. Well, adult kids—both of them just finished college." He laughed suddenly. "And there—Nathan brings two of the kids from Little League—they get to win tickets. Not by playing. I guess he channeled your dad. They get two backstage tickets for helping others to improve most. Kind of cool, huh?"

"Yep, very," Sky agreed. She smiled. The kids were in their midteens. Half grown-up—half not. They were watching everything that was going on wide-eyed and seemed thrilled when Charlie approached them, asking them to stand in different spots to make sure the revolving, colored lights looked good over the audience.

She glanced at the man with Julia. She'd never met him, but she assumed he had to be a relative or a family friend. Justin's marriage had always been solid as a rock, and she'd met Julia several times through the years. She was a woman who seemed to love what her husband did—and loved getting to see all the various performances he might work.

"Sky, did you want to take lead guitar on the ballad or just the vocals? I mean, you can do both, and I know that you might prefer both, but—"

"Brandon, can you take lead on that?" Sky asked. "I think I do want to concentrate on the vocals."

"Honored, Sky," Brandon assured her.

"Pulling in a wire!" Justin called, heading backstage right.

Sky couldn't help but notice that Chase idly followed him, stopping to talk briefly to Mark, check something on the drum set—and then head on back.

She wanted to follow, too.

But…

How did she do so without being obvious? Take a casual wander. Charlie was working with Joe, checking on the keyboard.

But as she moved, Mark was suddenly in front of her, grinning.

"You know, your dad really loved everyone. Different people for different reasons. Loved Roy Orbison's voice, the way Clapton could play… Who is your hero? Besides your dad, of course."

"And Skyhawk?" She smiled, looking back. She couldn't see Chase or Justin.

"Who else?"

"Um, hmm. Nancy Wilson, Heart! Killer voice. Oh—and I'm always a kid at heart. It wasn't live performance, but I loved, loved both Idina Menzel and Kristin Bell in *Frozen*. Wow. Hmm, oh, well—loved Idina Menzel from the get-go—saw *Wicked* on Broadway as a kid, and she was killing it then. And who wouldn't love Joan Jett? And I'll never forget Delores O'Riordan, beautiful voice! Seventies, hmm. Wow—how could anyone leave out Aerosmith? Journey?"

She kept smiling, talking.

How the hell could she casually get by him?

But…

Why would Chase be suspicious of Justin, of all people? Justin, great worker, solid as a rock, no overindulgences, great husband, great father…

But there was Julia, chatting now with the boys. Her friend, the stranger who had come with her, was just standing back, watching all the proceedings.

"Mark, Julia is here—Justin's wife. I'm going to go and talk to her, tell her that…that it's great to see her," she said.

"Oh, yeah, Julia! I'll come with you."

Great.

They both hopped off the stage, Mark turning to give Sky a hand. They walked over to Julia and the teen boys.

Sky barely got a chance to say hello before one of the kids said, "Wow, man, you're her! You're Skylar Ferguson."

She smiled. "Yes, I am. And thanks for being here. Oh! And I know how you got tickets to the show, so thanks for being such great young men."

They flushed, one speaking after the other, talking about Skyhawk numbers.

Julia looked uncomfortable. The strange man who was with her was watching.

He looked ready to move, almost ready to spring at any minute.

"Well, welcome, and we'll be seeing you!" Sky told the boys. "Julia, it's so great that you're here. Anyway, I just remembered I have to check to see if I brought clothes in for a change—"

"What you're wearing is cool. Love those jeans and that…shirt thing," one of the kids said.

"Tunic. It's a tunic," the other told him.

"Well, thank you, because at this point, if I did forget everything, it is what I'll be wearing!" she said.

Then she turned quickly, heading back to the stage, determined she was going to find out what Chase was doing.

And why Justin was…so strange.

"You need to…understand," Justin told Chase. The man was crying; tears were streaming down his face.

And he was terrified.

"I understand you're the one who managed to fray that wire. You were best friends with Jake, and you knew he'd be ready to do things himself to keep a show flowing smoothly. You knew he'd go to fix the amp."

"I…loved Jake!" he whispered.

And that was true; Chase believed him.

But something had clicked when they'd discovered that the places to drop off the money and to pick up the goods were right here.

And when he'd seen Justin…

He'd known. And he'd accused him in a straightforward manner when he'd gotten him alone, repeating the last words he'd heard Jake Ferguson say before he had died.

"I know what's going on and I saw... I'm going to put an end to it as soon as this gig is over!"

Justin caught his breath, trying to contain the violence of his sobs.

"He saw, he knew, and he was going to report you to the police. Because despite his own sobriety, Jake didn't mind others who could have a recreational drink or even a joint—what he minded was drugs being sold to children—and people dying!"

"I know, I know… I didn't care. I thought it would be over. They could arrest me—I didn't care about me. I had no choice. Then…or now…"

"Then, what the hell?" Chase exploded.

Justin looked toward the stage anxiously, trying to dry his face with his shirt sleeve, terrified as he looked toward the stage. "I never knew about the…fentanyl. That they are using it to cut hard drugs and handling it so recklessly. I didn't. I swear. But they got to me, they let me know, and even now—"

"Even now, what?" Chase demanded.

Justin looked at him. "If I don't—if *we* don't—walk back out there looking calm as can be, he's going to kill Julia. And as soon as word gets out, he's going to see that my boys are killed, too."

Chase stared at him. He had never believed that Justin was the head of their snake.

But just how deep did it run?

Back to the cartels theory. So who was the man with Julia today?

"All right, we'll talk quickly. Who is the man with your wife right now?"

"His name is Drew Carter. He's…been ordered to kill Julia if I don't make things happen the way that they're supposed to," Justin said.

"That's easy enough. I'll get out by him and—"

"No, no, he's just a…a pawn like me. His wife is in the hospital with a new baby. And there's a man there…ready to take her out along with the infant and…you don't know, you don't understand how bad all this is. And it's not just my wife. He's going to go after Sammy and Jeff—my sons. He's got them covered, too. Don't you see? There's no way out of this. He can kill anyone at any time with a snap of his fingers. His enforcers are everywhere."

"And so are the good guys and law enforcement," Chase told him.

"But if I don't—"

"You do what you're supposed to do. We're going to go through the show with you having done what you've been ordered to do. And by then…"

He broke off. He could see that Sky was coming into the wing.

"Hey!" she called cheerfully. But he knew Sky. She wanted to know what the hell was going on.

Did he dare tell her this was the man who had killed her beloved father?

"Can you get Wellington back here?" he asked her.

"Um, sure. But—"

"Now. Please."

"Sure. Okay."

She hurried back toward the stage. "Hey, Andy! Can

you come here for a minute? Chase wants to see what shirt you like best!"

Andy came on back quickly, excusing himself to the others. As he arrived, Chase told Sky, "Please, get back out there. Try to talk to Julia again and keep her with you."

"Why—"

"Please, please, just act normally, in a friendly manner." He looked at his watch. The doors would start opening in less than hour.

Whatever Justin was supposed to be doing, he was supposed to be doing it now.

The man still looked like hell. With Wellington there, he explained what he knew quickly, adding that Justin needed to get it together, to act as expected.

"My wife…the boys and…the others—"

"I'll get to the guy out there watching over Julia," Wellington promised. "Justin, do as Chase says—do what you're supposed to do. And don't be afraid. We'll get to your children before anyone else can."

"You don't understand how powerful—"

"Actually, I do. But you need to understand how powerful we can be when given the chance," Wellington told him. "I'll go have a discussion about lights with Drew Carter right now."

Wellington disappeared. Justin still looked like hell.

"Pull yourself together, man!" Chase ordered him. "This show has to go on as planned. All right, where does everything go?"

Justin shook his head. "There's not everything. I just put the money I got from the last haul—" He broke off, looking worse than he had. "Blood money," he said. "Right before we open the doors, I slip it beneath a particular seat, changes every time."

"Do you have your orders yet?"

"Yeah."

"And putting the money out was what Jake saw?"

"Yeah."

"And no one else ever saw you?" Chase asked.

He shrugged. "I just walk around the seat, look at the lights. Sometimes sit a few places. Everyone thinks I'm just checking it out."

"Do it. And quit crying. Justin, this truly has to be the performance of a lifetime for you."

"I'm not on stage. I head back to the wings. Then I get a message about where to find the stuff I'm supposed to distribute along with what I get to keep."

"Right now, come on. You can help salvage all the harm you've done. And you are performing now. All right. Go do your walkabout. Where exactly will you be putting it?"

"First balcony, front, center, dead center."

"And don't worry. In fact…"

He looked out. Wellington was standing with Julia, a laughing Sky and the man he'd been told was Drew Carter.

And he knew Wellington had seen to it that Carter knew it was over—and had given him everything he could possibly give him.

Agents would already be in the field.

They'd have the families safe. And they'd be watching. And waiting. Because when it was known that whatever lackey was the pickup man had been scooped, the so-called snake would probably see to it himself that his death threats against the families of those who had failed him had been carried out.

It was all a long shot.

And a real takedown might not happen. But Wellington would see to it that no innocents were harmed. Even if it meant giving up his own life.

But Wellington would be here tonight.

Watching. Waiting. And they all had to play it out.

"Justin? This all depends on you!" Chase said.

Justin straightened. "Yeah. I've got it. And I don't care what happens to me—"

"I know. Your family. I promise you, the people out there will see that they are safe. Justin, it's all in motion already. Just one more question before you start out. Who is the head of this thing?"

He shook his head miserably. "They call him El Rey."

El Rey.

Chase had heard the name before. And Wellington had been right. El Rey was really Miguel Esposito, head of one of the largest cartels, suspected to have slipped into the country illegally to take out a witness in a trial scheduled for just months ago.

No one had even imagined just how far this all reached.

"Showtime," he said.

SKY DIDN'T GET much of a chance to talk to Wellington, but she did know that he and Chase were working furiously at whatever it was that was going on.

And that Justin was involved somehow, and he'd been scared. No… Terrified.

But she had to have faith in the men. Her part in this was important, and her part was to get on stage, perform as she had never performed before, and make it all appear as if nothing was wrong at all, as if the world of rock 'n' roll was everything.

She saw the crew working quickly, leaving the audience, heading to the wings. Mark called out to her that they needed to get back, that the MC would be taking over the booth.

Wellington had Julia and Drew Carter somewhere—she didn't know where. But she had a feeling a few of the extra crew members were his men.

That Wellington was a man with the power to make things happen quickly.

"Heads up!" It was Kenneth Malcolm calling out. "House lights up! Doors are open!"

He was in the wings, impeccable as usual in a casual beige suit. Sky couldn't help but wonder about him.

After all, other than the three who worked specifically for Skyhawk and those who worked for other bands, Kenneth Malcolm was the man who did the hiring.

He had hired Bobby Sacks.

But Bobby Sacks had been a victim.

She wondered bitterly how anyone, including a drug kingpin, could expect anyone to keep payments coming in, taking the big deliveries from him to disperse for the megamoney to be gained on the streets, when the customers were dying from the product.

But she doubted that whoever was behind it all cared. Could a man like Kenneth Malcolm have been involved? How could he and still keep his job?

Then again, who knew the venue the way he did?

Mark and Joe were laughing together as they headed stage right; Chris was behind them, reminding Brandon which numbers he wanted him sitting in for. Sky naturally reminded him where she wanted him to take lead guitar and, of course, he should stay on backup vocals through the whole show, if he wanted, although he probably knew them all as well as she did, if not better.

She didn't see Justin; Nathan was heading stage right with them while Charlie was heading stage left.

Curtains were opened as people continued coming in.

Lights on the stage blazed as they did so, people in twos and threes and larger groups, loud and excited as they came in, some with drinks and snacks, others just anxious to find their seats.

The MC spoke over backup music as the crowd came in, talking about the show, the weather, the city, welcoming everyone.

Every seat was filled when he announced, "And now, ladies and gentlemen, boys and girls, and whoever! Let's welcome to the stage, Skyhawk!"

It was time to make their entry.

Skyhawk. Her father's creation, the music, his love. And tonight, Skyhawk was the three older rockers, Chris Wiley, Mark Reynolds and Joe Garcia, still looking the part, agile, vibrant for their ages, long hippie hair, and all that they needed to be.

And then her, Brandon and Chase. Second and third generations.

Skyhawk, changing, growing—and yet the embodiment of love that her dad had created.

Her part in all that was just to play with all her heart.

They ran out, waving to everyone and going for their instruments, Chase bowing broadly as his name was shouted, grinning and then maintaining a fantastic drumroll.

They burst straight into one of Skyhawk's most popular

numbers, "The Path I Took," and from there, they moved straight into one of her dad's older ballads.

Act normal, behave normally, give the show all your heart and…

Trust in Chase, in Wellington, and that everything is being handled. Her part was to keep this moving, give them the opportunity to do what was needed…

"Welcome! We are Skyhawk, and we're thrilled to be here, thrilled to have you here with us! I'm Sky Ferguson, and you have known Chris Wiley, Mark Reynolds and Joe Garcia for—"

"Decades!" Joe put in dryly, bringing a bout of laughter to the crowd.

"We have Chase McCoy on drums tonight—though Hank has told him he wants his place back as soon as possible! But we'll make do, right?"

Her words were greeted with laughter and another round of phenomenal drumming.

Chase, too, was playing his part.

"We also have Brandon Wiley with us tonight, and this guy does just about everything!"

Brandon created a combo of melodies quickly, then they moved into a fast, heavy rock piece that had once ruled the airwaves.

She moved about the stage, forgetting she'd told Chase she wouldn't carry the mic. But her father had moved; it was natural, swirling and dancing while doing the songs, the numbers she had known since she was a small child…

Songs she had done with her dad. And she gave it her heart as she went along, because as serious as the night had become, it was also her ode to him.

Mark stepped in when it was time to take a break, announcing with her that they were giving everyone a chance to head out for drinks, snacks and merchandise. Hey, the place was in it for the money, right?

They could bring the crowd to laughter and applause, and it felt good.

Even if…

Running to the stage-right wing, she found herself crashing into Chase's arms.

"Our guys have the families!" he whispered to her, pretending to nuzzle her ear. "Kids, wives, good… They went in the back. They'll be waiting."

She smiled at him, pretending to whisper in his ear as well.

"Ah, lovebirds!" Mark said. "It's adorable to see you two together again."

"I'm adorable?" Chase asked, grinning.

It was going the best that it could. But she didn't see Justin anywhere. She knew he had to be playing whatever part it was that he needed to, but…

She managed to slide back into his arms and ask softly, "Justin?"

"He's good. Agent at his side."

She nodded. They weren't playing, but the canned music and the noise of the crowd was almost deafening, still. They waited, talking about where they were going next. Mark and Joe reminded her of the songs they would do for the encore; it was apparent that this crowd would demand it.

Then the MC announced the return of Skyhawk to the stage. It was time to run back out there.

Next…

Drum solos, songs that featured each instrument and

each player. A wonderful crowd in the audience, cheering them on, moments when she needed to chat, to laugh, to draw the others in, moving across the stage, covering the stage…

And all the while wondering what was going on, how Chase, too, was managing to bang away, come in with drumrolls when she was about to speak, to bring them back to their performance, to follow her as she crossed the stage, paused to make comments to those off the apron by the stage…

Then she thanked everyone for coming. For supporting Skyhawk.

She thanked them for having loved her dad and all the music he had created.

Then they were running off stage, listening, waiting, hearing the crowd roar, screaming that they come back, and then the MC announcing they'd return for the last few songs…

Her father's songs. Songs about life, learning about the dark side and how to find the light, about love, about the strength to be found in the eyes of a loved one…

Then it was done.

"Thank you! Skyhawk thanks you, I thank you, and among the angels—trust me!—my dad thanks you!"

She ran back offstage. Show over. Encore over. And…

She stood with the others in the wings, just breathing, as the MC announced safe paths out, as crowds of people began to leave from the floor, from the balconies.

Chase was right next to her; she had a feeling he wouldn't be leaving her.

Justin was nowhere to be seen.

Neither was his wife, nor the man who had been with her.

She looked at Chase, but he evidently didn't intend to say anything at that moment, other than to join in the happy banter that was going around, everyone congratulating each other on the success of the show.

Andy Wellington was not backstage.

The teenage boys were, and a few other special guests. A few reporters, a few photographers, but all of them gleaning and snapping what they could.

And finally, Chase whispered to her, "Let's escape to a dressing room!"

She nodded, feeling his arm around her, leading her.

But a man with a recorder stopped them.

"Ferguson and McCoy, together again!" he said.

Chase smiled and looked at Sky. "Were we ever really apart?" he asked.

"Aw, man, but now…will you two be continuing with the band?" the reporter asked.

"Oh, well, the band…the main members of Skyhawk were friends before they were the band—our families have been friends. We've been friends. I'm sure we will be playing together again. When, where and how often, well, that will remain to be seen."

"Skylar, you work with kids—"

"Kids and music," she said, glancing up at Chase.

She wanted to talk to him alone!

"Okay, Chase, so, we understand that you've been working in a number of labs, that you've gotten into forensic sciences. Will that continue into your future?"

Chase laughed easily. "Right now, our future is getting home—we have a new dog! So, hey, thank you, thanks so much for your interest, but…"

"We're just dead tired!" Sky said.

She winced inwardly, wishing she hadn't used the word *dead.*

Chase was already leading her away. "Thank you! Thank you so much for your interest in Skyhawk!"

He managed to get her to one of the dressing rooms, pushing the door open and then leaning against it, shaking his head.

"Chase, what's going on?" she asked.

"Wellington is a good man and good at what he does. He had agents with Justin's family—and with Drew Carter's—before we were halfway through the first set. Now…he's got people trying to get the place cleared out while following whoever goes for the money. We need to just sit tight for a minute and wait—"

His phone buzzed, and he looked at it quickly. "They've got something. Stay here, don't move. Keep the door locked. Don't answer it to anyone—*anyone*—but me."

"Chase, I—"

"Please, Sky, I'm begging you, just listen to me right now."

She nodded.

He slipped out. She locked the door.

And she knew that every second would seem like an hour until he returned.

Chapter Nine

The houses were covered; agents were waiting. Justin was safe, Julia was safe…

But something had happened. What should have been an easy and clear operation had changed when the lackey picking up the funds Justin had left managed to sense the agents about to nab him. The place had been almost clear, but a woman with a teenage girl had been just exiting when the man doing the pickup had grabbed her and the kid. He threatened to throw them off the balcony, and law enforcement had backed off, giving him time for an agile leap down to the sound booth, onto the floor and up again onto the stage and into the wings.

He was back there now, joining the friends, reporters and others who grouped backstage after a performance.

Chase sped through the wings, seeking anyone who matched the poor description that they had so far. White, medium height, medium build, brown hair.

And, it seemed, they were hiring their lackeys from the ranks of acrobats—he should have broken a leg attempting his escape route.

But he had made it. And in the arena where there were still a few people milling about, the agents had refrained from firing so they wouldn't hit an innocent or worse, create a panic that would allow the perpetrator even greater leeway.

Chase stepped from the dressing room just in time to see the door to the performers' parking lot begin to swing closed.

He took off, slamming it back open, racing into the back.

He saw a man. Medium height and build. Brown hair.

He tore after him; he was in decent shape himself, but contrary to what he saw on TV most of the time, he hadn't been in that many situations where a perp had run.

But he was after him in a flash.

This guy could run.

"Stop!" Chase shouted.

The man turned to look back—and in doing so, he tripped, thankfully. Chase didn't think that he could have outrun him.

But he was on the ground, moaning. Chase reached him, dug plastic cuffs from his wallet and dragged him to his feet.

He frowned as he did so. The man didn't seem to have packets or…anything.

And, as Chase looked at him, he started to laugh.

"You'll never beat a king, you know."

"You handed it off!" Chase said.

"Me? I didn't do a thing. In fact…hey, you're the damned drummer. Cool. I can sue the venue, the promoters—and Skyhawk!"

"Oh, I don't think so!"

Chase pushed the man along before him, wishing he'd gotten set up with earbuds and a mic, but that hadn't been feasible when he'd been playing the drums, and he had to keep one hand on the guy while he used the other to call Wellington.

"I've got him, but he's passed it off!"

"Get him in here."

"He's suing us all," Chase said dryly.

"I don't think so. Too many witnesses, and I'm willing to bet he's got a rap sheet a mile long. Who did he pass it off to?"

"I don't know—"

"Back on lockdown. Now!" Wellington said. "Agents ready to get him—"

"I have to get back in—Sky—"

"Agents at the door. Hand him over—get to Sky."

"On it."

He ended his call, dragging the man back toward the stage doors.

"He's going to shoot your ass, you know."

"Who is?"

"The king."

"Well, he can try. What's the king's name?"

"It's *King*, obviously," the man said.

"What's your name?"

"Myron."

"Myron what?"

"Myron Mouse. What the hell. Hey, I want an attorney."

"That will all be arranged for you."

"You should stick to the drums. Now I'm just suing you personally!"

"Yeah, go for it!"

Chase was finally getting him back toward the rear-stage doors. As Wellington had promised, the door opened, and two agents appeared. He knew the one man—he'd worked with him before in Baton Rouge in a small sting at a bar. He was Gene Shepherd, another agent who worked a lot of undercover cases and was excellent at sliding into just about any group anywhere.

He and his companion, an attractive female agent, were casually dressed. He was wearing a Skyhawk T-shirt while she was dressed in jeans and a soft, light sweater—but one bulky enough that he knew she was armed beneath it. They'd naturally been filtered into the audience and looked the part of any couple heading to a rock concert.

"Got him," Shepherd assured them. "Hey, cool, thanks, we weren't expecting this kind of help from a drummer."

"Hey, he's trying to ruin what was a good concert. And he might be an accessory to murder," Chase said.

"Murder! I didn't murder anyone!" the man protested. "Hey, I wasn't here when Jake Ferguson was killed!"

"Who knows what laws we can make stick?" Shepherd asked. "Good prosecutor, a jury tired of drugs killing people—"

"I didn't kill anyone!" he protested again. "No one is dead—"

"Yeah, people are dead and dying from that stuff you sold," Chase told him.

"I didn't sell it! The king sold it. I mean, maybe someone got carried away. Look, I don't make the stuff. I don't package the stuff. I'm a messenger, that's all. I'm told to get drop-offs, nothing else. I didn't kill anyone, I didn't. Wait! Not only did I not kill anyone—I didn't do a damned thing. There's no money on me, nothing—you need to let me go this instant. Brutality! Oh, hell, yeah, I am going to have a field day with you in court!"

"We'll see," Shepherd said. "Chase, you can—"

"You idiots! I'll be out on bail in an hour. And when I'm out, you're going to be so sorry! You're going to wish for death before you get to that sweet peace—"

"He's threatening us now," Shepherd said. "I'm pretty sure that death threats are illegal in themselves. Man, we've got him on so much!"

"You have nothing!"

"Enough to see that a jury puts you away forever and ever. Then again, this is Louisiana, and if it weren't, we're federal, and sometimes—" Shepherd said.

"You're threatening me! Wait until I talk to my lawyer!"

"You'll get a lawyer," Shepherd promised.

"Yeah, you will," Chase said, but he took the man by the shoulders, spinning him around to stare at him and demand, "Who did you pass it off to?"

A shot suddenly rang out. It missed the man by about half an inch.

Chase threw himself on the suspect, bringing them both down flat. Shepherd and his companion were already down, weapons drawn, and Shepherd was speaking into his body mic.

"Shots fired! Sniper in the rear-stage parking!"

Chase dragged the culprit behind a dumpster along with Shepherd and his partner.

"Your king will be happy to kill you! If it was me, I'd be throwing myself on the mercy—and safety—of law enforcement!" Chase told him.

"No, no, they were aiming at you!"

"Were they?" Chase asked. "You know that isn't true. You failed. You're a liability now. Better off dead to those who pay you. Who the hell did you give the packet to?" he demanded again. "Hey, we'll fight for your life, but..."

The lackey must have known that his so-called king killed anyone who failed him, because he suddenly started shaking.

"You don't understand—"

"Oh," Shepherd said, "with your crowd, failure is death. So maybe you want to join a new crowd. We can keep you safe."

"He has a long reach. Even in prison."

"Solitary confinement. You can live. Maybe one day, the king and his royalty will be gone, and you can have a life again," Shepherd's partner said quietly.

"All right, all right!"

He told them who he had given the packet to.

And Chase was stunned. He might have known. He might have suspected.

But still…

"I've got to get back in!" he said.

"We'll cover you," Shepherd assured him.

Chase leaped to his feet, diving for the door. It was still wedged open, and he ripped it the rest of the way, sliding behind its protection as quickly as he could.

A shot rang out.

But as Shepherd and his partner returned fire, the door closed behind Chase.

He was in.

He had to get back to Skylar.

"SKYLAR!"

She heard her name being anxiously called just seconds after Chase left.

"Skylar, Skylar Ferguson! It's Special Agent Brent Masters. Wellington sent me to get you out of here. I can show you my credentials."

"Chase said to wait for him!"

"No, it's all gone to hell. There's been a pass-off, and we have to get you the hell out of here. Now. Look…look through the little hole. You can see my credentials."

There was a peephole in the dressing-room door. She looked through it. The credentials looked real enough. But…

"I have been ordered to get you to safety!" the man said.

There had been a pass-off?

"Aw, hell, Miss Ferguson…"

She heard a key rattling.

This guy had the keys to the dressing rooms. She prayed that made him real.

The door opened. He looked enough like an agent. But maybe he looked like a drug smuggler, too.

"Come on, please, Wellington is across the stage, and he knows Chase is out and wants you with him. I'm the real deal, I swear it—"

He never finished his sentence. She never saw the person who slammed his head with a guitar, sending him crashing down to the floor.

Out like a light.

But then she did see who had wielded the weapon. And to her astonishment, it was someone who hadn't dressed to blend in with a bunch of rockers.

It was Kenneth Malcom, and as usual, he was dressed impeccably in one of his suits.

"Skylar, that guy was a phony. He thought he'd knocked me out over there, and he stole my master key… Let me get you to Wellington before another of these perps gets over here!"

Wellington had filled the place with undercover agents.

But it seemed that head of the drug cartel or whoever was pulling the strings had filled it with his own people as well.

"Come on!" he told her anxiously. "Skylar, hurry, I owe it to your dad to make sure that you're safe!"

She looked at the man on the floor; he was out.

If nothing else, Kenneth Malcom knew how to play the guitar as weapon.

"Skylar!"

She followed him out. The dressing rooms were stage left while most of the workings of any show there took place stage right.

"We'll head around the back. You don't see anyone, right?"

She shook her head, hurrying by him, ready to run across the back of the stage until she met the one man that she knew Chase trusted entirely.

But she had barely gotten around the back before she saw Chris Wiley coming her way, looking anxious.

"Skylar! Thank God. Brandon is going around the other way for you. Seems Chase headed on out, getting himself involved in all this—"

"Chris," Kenneth Malcolm exploded from behind her. "You! You're the one. You saw to it that Justin was played because you knew that he loved his wife and kids more than his own life. Get the hell away from her now, Chris."

"What?" Chris demanded.

"You heard me, move aside. I'm getting her out of here!"

Brandon appeared then, coming from the other direction. "Thank God! You found her. Skylar—"

"Both of you! Back off, you bastard pushers, get away from her."

"Kenneth, what in God's name is wrong with you?" Chris demanded. "Leave her alone. Let Skylar come with us right away, and go and do whatever the hell you need to be doing—getting out of here yourself, getting to safety—"

"Move. Now. I don't trust you—either of you," Malcolm said.

"Malcolm!" Brandon exploded.

Sky stood there, torn, incredulous.

And not at all sure who to trust.

"Let me just go back to the dressing room!" she said. "All of you, leave me alone. I'll be with Chase soon enough, and you guys can argue this out with the agents—"

"Where's the agent? The guy who was going to get Skylar?" Chris demanded.

"There was no agent—just another pusher who was better disguised," Malcolm said. "Now, I mean it, you two, get the hell out of the way."

Chris Wiley shook his head. "Jake Ferguson was my best friend and, however it played out, you had something to do with him dying. You get the hell out of my way, and you get the hell away from Skylar!"

Chris and Brandon stood together, staring at Sky and Malcolm, hands on their hips, determined.

She couldn't believe it.

Chris had been one of her father's best friends. And Brandon was far from a perfect human being, but they were all far from perfect.

And Kenneth Malcolm…

She turned. And she turned just in time to see him smile and reach behind his back, under his always-perfect jacket, and produce a gun.

"Sorry, Skylar, I was going to try to make this a little easier for you… I really do like your father's songs and the way that you do them, but…"

"Let her go!" Chris demanded. "What, are you going to shoot me, with FBI agents running all over the place?"

"Uh, yeah, no problem."

Kenneth Malcolm fired, and Chris went down and before she could run to him, Malcolm had his hands on her, fingers through her hair, dragging her with him and away from the fallen man and his stricken son.

She let out a scream that could have wakened the dead, but Kenneth Malcolm shouted almost as loudly.

"One more sound out of you and I shoot Brandon, too!"

He aimed at Brandon.

She gritted her teeth, stared at him and said, "Don't you dare—lead the damned way!"

And he did, lifting a ring in the floor and forcing her down a ladder ahead of him.

CHASE HEARD SKYLAR'S scream just as the door slammed shut behind him. He hurried toward the sound and was just in time to see that Chris Wiley was on the ground, bleeding, with Brandon hovering over him, screaming for help.

He paused by Chris, hitting a speed dial that instantly brought Wellington's voice to his ear.

"Man down, we need an ambulance, now," Chase said.

"It's a flesh wound," Chris groaned. "Go, go, go—he's got Skylar."

"Malcolm?"

"He threatened to shoot me, too, if Sky didn't move. She basically told him to go to hell, but…she moved. She wouldn't let him shoot me," Brandon said.

"Please…"

There was no pretense going on anymore; Chase could hear sirens blazing through the night.

"Chris, they're on the way—"

"I'm fine. My shoulder…well, hell, it's good I'm not the drummer!" Chris said.

"Where?"

"Into the floor."

"The floor—a trapdoor, there!" Brandon said, pointing it out. Chase had to admit he hadn't even thought about a stage basement. They didn't use it for their rock shows; when theatrical performances were put on, characters and set pieces could be moved up and down.

He nodded, feeling like an idiot, hurrying to the spot where there was a small metal ring that brought up a three-by-three piece of the flooring, revealing a ladder.

He moved down it cautiously, quickly speaking with Wellington, advising him as to his position and letting him know that the man had Sky.

Only dim light filtered through from above. No one had thought about the area—it wasn't being used.

But then, maybe they'd figured this would just be too simple. Wait and see who was picking up the goods and nab them after making sure that threatened families were safe.

He should have known better. Nothing in life was ever easy. He shouldn't have left Skylar, but if he hadn't…

They would never know that there had been a pass-off, that there were more people involved here than they had imagined.

Malcolm. Chase had thought of him. But he'd also set his name aside because he hadn't been at the other venues. Apparently, this whole thing was bigger than even Wellington had imagined.

He reached the ground. The area was empty, other than a few large storage containers. He drew a penlight from his pocket, desperately searching.

If they had come down here, where the hell—

He saw a panel to his left and determined that it had to slide, lead somewhere.

It did.

Across the area to the rear of the stage, beyond, and to another ladder that led up to…the door backstage. The one he had come through. The one in lockdown now…

But Kenneth Malcolm was the one who managed the venue. The one who had probably studied the blueprints a zillion times over.

He was the one person who would know how to silence alarms and bypass a lockdown.

Swearing, he ripped open the door, heedless of the sound that instantly keened through the venue. The cops were there.

Agents were there. All good men and women, steady people who knew their jobs…

But hadn't known Kenneth Malcolm.

SKYLAR HAD NEVER been below the stage, and she didn't know what to expect once they went down the ladder.

But once they were away from others, she didn't intend to be so obliging.

"Move!" Malcolm told her.

"I'm moving. What? Do you want me to break a leg and slow you down even more, you idiot? And you are an idiot. Now everyone is going to know who you are and what you did—"

"And no one will give a damn when I'm on a beach in Mexico!" he promised her.

"Oh, am I going to Mexico?"

He started to laugh. "Skylar Ferguson, child of Jake, beloved by all, little nightingale, and now… Well, you guys were good tonight. You know, there are probably a thousand men out there who would love to take you to Mexico! But I'm no fool. You'd kill me the first chance you got."

"Because you're the one who ordered Justin to fix the amp that killed my father," she said flatly.

"No, it was my suggestion, and I was the one on the dark web that gave the order—promising to see that Julia and the kids were killed if he failed—but I'm not the be-all and end-all," he said. "But you look like such a beautiful, sweet thing. I know, however, that you're a raving bitch."

"So what's the deal? You're going to kill me, too?" she asked.

"Not quite yet, not if you try to be a good girl."

"If you're going to kill me anyway, why would I be a good girl?"

"Because there's always hope, right? You can live on the hope that your boy toy will make it to you somehow, or one of his lecturing friends." He laughed. "Hope that you move and that your idiot drummer boy doesn't pop up in front of me, threatening me."

"If not insurance against such a thing, what am I?"

"Okay, you are insurance. But seriously, try to be nice,

Skylar. I know you can do it. I've seen you with other people. So behave…"

"I see. You're taking me so you can get to Mexico. I hate to tell you, but it's not going to work."

"And why would that be?"

"They'll shoot down your plane."

"No, they'd kill an innocent pilot. They don't want to do that, right?"

She started to laugh suddenly. "And you think you have a plan that will get you to a plane and off the ground and no one is going to know? You're an idiot—"

"That's not being nice," he warned, thrusting the nose of the gun against her skull.

"Well, you are. If you hadn't come for me, you could have walked out on your own, and no one would have noticed."

"No, that fool knew. He knew when he saw me with the packet."

"The fool? You mean the real FBI agent who came to the dressing-room door."

"He would have told Wellington. I had to take him down, and I'm not sure I killed him, and there you were, so…now you're insurance. And again—"

"Okay, so I'm going with you to a car. Whose car? How—"

"You don't need to worry about whose car."

"Oh, I see. The idiot who picked up the package passed it on to you when he realized that he was seen and being chased. And the FBI agent saw the exchange. And with all the metal detectors, no one other than law-enforcement officials should have had firearms, but you didn't need to bring a firearm in because you'd already stashed one here for emergencies."

"So smart. Wow. A real Einstein."

They were still on the ground. It was dark, but she could see the hatred in his eyes as he shoved her.

"Move, Einstein."

"Where?"

"The panel, you dolt."

"Hey, I've never had an occasion to be down here before!"

"That's right. You horrible, elitist, wretched, conceited performers! You think that you walk on stage and the world adores you. You don't give a damn about anyone working—you just want your music, your drinks and your drugs, and your good old rock 'n' roll."

"That's bull. My father cared about everyone. He cared about kids being given drugs, and he's turning over in his grave right now because you're killing people everywhere with drugs that aren't just addictive, they're lethal—"

"Oh, no, no. I'm just this venue. The king has many subjects. Now, get the hell through the panel."

Sky moved toward it. He reached past her to shove it open.

If she pushed him, if she went for his arm…

"Don't even think about it," he told her.

She pushed the panel, went through the door. They started to move up to the main level again, reaching the door to the backstage parking.

"An alarm will raise all hell. If you just go and leave me—"

"Not on your life!"

"But—"

"You forget. I run this place," he reminded her, smiling grimly.

Of course.

He hit a code in a box by the door and pushed it open. The door silently moved, and they stepped outside.

There were agents everywhere!

Except out here.

Because, of course, they'd had the place locked down. The agents were approaching, questioning and perhaps even searching everyone.

Somewhere busy talking to Chris and Brandon and others…

No. They would know. Brandon would have told them about the entry to the lower-stage area and they would be coming after her…

"Hey!" someone shouted.

But Kenneth Malcolm didn't hesitate. He turned, taking a wild shot, not really caring if it hit its target or not.

They heard the sound of a thud. Someone had hit the ground.

And there was no fire in return.

"So you just killed another innocent?"

"Maybe I just wounded a bastard cop. No time to figure it out."

"After all this, you think your king is going to get you to Mexico? I hear he kills people who don't carry out all his plans."

"I'm not just a flunky."

"Hmm. That could be all the worse!"

"Shut the hell up and move. Over there. That nice little SUV that looks like every other SUV and has the dirtied plates. I am not an idiot, Miss Ferguson. I'm a smart man—the one who will kill you if he has to."

She moved ahead as he prodded her with the gun, praying that whoever had called out to him wasn't dead.

Chase would come after her. She knew it.

But she knew, as well, that she needed to keep herself alive. He'd pointed out that she had no training.

But she had instinct, and she desperately wanted this man brought to justice, to pay for what he had done to her father and others.

She had to watch and wait because…

He would make a mistake. She didn't know when or where, but he would make a mistake.

And when he did, she swore silently to herself, she would be ready.

She had wanted the truth. She had wanted it so badly because there should be no disbelief, no skepticism ever, that her father had found his focus in life, that he had never fallen again, that he had lived for his music—and for others.

She closed her eyes, remembering him. He'd had such strength and such courage. Seeing him, in her mind's eye, in her memories, she knew that he had served his country and more, and he had lived every day of his life with courage, the courage to be his own man, the best husband and the best father.

He had given her music. And so much more.

And this…

Whatever happened, she would face it, manage it, do what she could…

This man had caused her father's death. She wouldn't falter. And with faith in his memory, and men like Chase, she just might make it. And who knew? Others knew that Malcolm had taken her.

Chase knew.

Malcolm had told her about hope. Hope was good to cling to. Hope, courage…and faith.

She had been lucky in life because the men in her life had all three. She would have all three, too.

Chapter Ten

Chase burst out the rear-stage door.

At first, he saw nothing, no one. Then he heard a groan, and he hurried over to the dumpster.

He found another man down and recognized him as Victor Suarez, again, a man he knew to be a good agent.

His eyes were closed; he didn't appear to be moving. But he'd made a sound, and that meant that he had to be alive. Chase called Wellington as he hunkered down, telling him they needed med techs outside as soon as possible. He checked for the man's pulse; his heart was still beating.

His eyes fluttered.

"Black…black SUV," he muttered. "Plates…"

"Hey, help is coming," Chase told him, searching for the injury that had caused the large stain on his lower right gut. He ripped a piece of his shirt, pressing the wound, knowing that the blood flow had to be stopped. "Can you hold this?" he asked. "Victor, the bleeding…"

Suarez nodded and placed his hand on the pressure dressing Chase had created. He pressed down himself.

"Got…it."

"Can you tell me… You said 'plates.' What about the plates?" Chase asked.

"O-obscured," the man said. "Muddied. On purpose, I'd bet. He has her…she's…"

"Hurt? Is she hurt?"

The man on the ground moved his mouth. No sound came, but he formed the word *no.*

Then he winced and managed to open his eyes, looking up at Chase. "Go! You've—you've got help coming. I think… I was a damned idiot, warning him…should have shot him flat out. No, right, we are the law, we don't just commit murder, but…"

Black SUV, plates obscured.

The man's eyes opened again. "Mic and buds…take my mic. Easier…"

"Thanks, thank you!"

Brilliant idea. He reached gently for the little button on the man's collar and even more lightly for the buds in his ears.

"Wellington, have you—"

"Got you loud and clear. And help is there. EMTs are headed out the door right now."

"Thanks. I see them, and I'm heading out after Sky. She may have her phone in her pocket, and he may not have thought of it if she didn't pull it out. Can you—"

"You bet. I'll get a trace on the location."

"Thanks. I'm heading out."

"Listen, I can get a trace on her phone going, but it will take me a few minutes. You can hold position—"

"No. I've got something else I have to do quickly," Chase said suddenly. "Get back to me, please, as soon as possible."

The med techs had arrived, and Chase stood, nodded to them and took off. His car was just a few feet away.

There was only one exit from the passenger lot, but he needed to think.

Where the hell would the man be going?

But first things first: he was going to take a lightning-quick side trip. Sky's place was close.

If it came to a point where he might need help…

There might be no better help than some he had quickly available to him.

He was out and moving in seconds. At Sky's house, he was grateful he knew the code as well as he knew his own.

He was in and out in seconds with Larry at his heels.

"Now, boy, where did he take her? He should be calling, asking for money, demanding clearance to get away… something. Unless…"

The *unless* was just grim. She might be a human shield for him, insurance, a hostage for bargaining.

Where? Esposito was still somewhere—he hadn't gone to the homes where he had sent his assassins to take care of the families of the men who had failed him.

Would he welcome Kenneth Malcolm, anyway?

As he anxiously asked himself questions, he heard Wellington's voice. "You're right, Chase, she's got her phone on her. He's heading west, out of the city. There's a small airport there… He's no good to his cartel king anymore, but he's got a major payoff on him, and there's a small airport—"

"I know it," Chase told him quickly. "I know exactly where it is."

"Sending backup."

"Fast as you can."

"We've got the control tower. They'll stall on the plane."

"Gotcha. Thanks."

He turned toward the highway, glad he knew the city and the route to take.

Grateful, too, when Wellington's voice came to him again.

"He had one hell of a lead, but you're closing in. The airport is right ahead—"

"Yeah. I know."

"Backup—"

"May be too late. Still no sign of Miguel—"

"No. As I told you, the families are safe. Agents got his assassins, and I think one of them is a major player. That part of the takedown went as planned—even though we were hoping these were hits the man might have wanted to take himself." He was silent just a moment and added, "We should have been on Malcolm," Wellington said.

"*I* should have been on him," Chase said, furious with himself that he had missed the man. But they hadn't known the scope of what was happening.

Now they did.

"Half a mile. I think they're turning into the airport."

"Yeah."

Chase was on them. They *were* turning into the small airport. But he knew that if Malcolm saw him, he'd probably shoot Sky on the spot just to kill her, because he wouldn't go down alone.

He drove the car to the side of the road, drew his weapon and warned Larry, "Stay close to me! Duty, Larry. We're on duty."

Larry gave a little sound of agreement. He'd been trained in many disciplines and was still a police dog to the core.

Chase leaped over the small fence, followed by Larry,

and they headed along the outer shell of the place, watching as the black SUV came to a halt.

"Stealth mode, Larry," he said.

He hadn't had much of a chance to work with the dog, but he had faith that Sky had been given one of the best, an animal deserving a good life after taking a few shots in the line of duty.

Creeping along the buildings, they came within earshot as Malcolm got out of the car.

Sky apparently had no intention of helping him. He walked around to the passenger's seat, searching the area as he did so, grabbing her arm and dragging her out of the car.

"Now!" he told her harshly.

Larry was tense, letting out a low growl.

"Steady, boy, steady. On my command," Chase told him.

He could hear Sky. She wasn't rolling over—or shaking in fear.

"Why? You said you didn't want to take me to Mexico!" she said harshly.

Malcolm was looking at the plane, frowning. "Where the hell's the damned pilot?" He drew his gun, looking around.

As he asked the question, a man appeared at the top of the short flight of stairs leading to the body of the jet.

It wasn't the pilot.

Chase had never seen him in person before, but he'd seen pictures on the screens at the New Orleans offices.

It was Miguel Esposito, head of the major crime ring behind it all.

"So, here you are!" Esposito said to Malcolm. "And with a hostage. You have the money?"

"Right here," Malcolm told him. "Yeah, I've got a hostage."

"So…who do we have here?"

"Just a disposable, as soon as we get the bird in the air free and clear."

"Ah, but maybe not so quickly!" Esposito said, eyeing Sky with amusement.

"Disposable, trust me. She's trouble," Malcolm said.

"But so are you. You screwed the pooch, Malcolm. We lost major players."

"That wasn't me!" Malcolm told him. "Idiots—"

"Idiots you dragged into the ring, *mi amigo*."

"I've got the money. The operation wasn't going to run forever. I did my part."

Malcolm was dragging Sky to the plane, looking back to see if anyone was coming.

"Well, we have a long flight in which to discuss the future," Esposito said. "For now…send up the *chica*!"

Chase quickly weighed his options—and his chances. Sky was with two men who were hardened killers, both armed. While it would be one hell of a thing to bring down Esposito, Sky was his priority. If he shot, he had to do so damned fast: kill one, the other might instantly aim at her and…

Esposito turned back into the plane. Malcolm was forcing Sky up the small set of stairs.

But Sky was apparently going for broke. Even though Malcolm held his weapon loosely in his hand.

Maybe she knew that Malcolm would eventually have

his way. That Esposito might have fun with her for a bit, but eventually…

She wasn't suicidal, Chase knew.

But she was no one's patsy.

She spun suddenly, quicker than lightning, slamming a knee into Malcolm so hard that he teetered on the first step behind her and started to fall. And Sky was ready to pounce, ready to fly for the gun he was holding.

But she might not make it.

Chase wasn't alone: he had Larry.

He fired.

His aim was true. He caught Malcolm dead center in the back of the head, and the man went down.

Esposito reappeared, gun out. He didn't know what had happened, but he was ready to take on the woman who had already leaped down the last steps and ducked behind the ladder in hopes of reaching for Malcolm's weapon which had now flown just steps away…

But Esposito didn't see her right away. Of course, he would have known from the sound of the shot that it had been fired from a distance.

"Now, boy, now!"

Larry went running out for his new mistress, barking and growling furiously.

Esposito was distracted, trying to take aim at a dog that seemed to have the speed of a greyhound.

Chase stepped out where he could be seen.

Esposito whirled around, taking aim at him then.

Not fast enough.

Chase had known exactly where he was aiming, and with Esposito determined to fire, he had no choice.

He fired himself. The king went down. Sky emerged from her ducking stance beneath the steps.

Larry threw himself at her, and she almost fell backward again, taking the giant pup into her arms. She soothed the dog, assuring him she was all right, and stared at Chase incredulously.

He ran toward her, just as an explosion of sirens burst into the air, and the backup he'd been promised came barreling through the gates to the private airfield.

SKY COULDN'T SPEAK as she held Larry, and Chase came to take them both into his arms. She'd been thinking that she was an idiot—when she'd been thinking at all. Fear had all but paralyzed her when she'd seen that she wasn't up against just one man with a gun but two.

And still…

She wasn't going to be taken. She wasn't going to be tortured before she was killed. There had been no choice. Her plan had been to throw Kenneth Malcolm off so badly that she'd seriously injure him and grab the gun and then duck under the plane until she got a chance to either *try* to shoot the other man or somehow escape.

She'd thought she had a chance.

Because while she might have been *disposable*, she was certain that, to the man on the plane, Kenneth Malcolm was equally disposable. And whoever the other man had been, Malcolm had caused him some considerable trouble. Considering the consequences, if Kenneth Malcolm was down, he might have shrugged it off and left without her.

No. Probably not. But there was always hope, even if it hadn't done too much for Malcolm.

She'd prayed that help might be coming…

How, she wasn't sure. But Chris and Brandon had known that Malcolm had her and…

"Oh, my God!" She found speech at last, pulling away from Chase and asking him desperately, "You got Larry. You and Larry—but, oh! Chase! Chris! Chris Wiley. He was shot, and a man in the parking lot—"

"They are being taken care of. I truly believe they're both going to make it," Chase assured her. "Skylar…oh, God, Skylar!"

"You came in time!" she told him. "How…?"

She loved the smile that touched his lips. "Well, Larry and I were pretty good. But you, Skylar Ferguson, gave us what we needed when you fought for yourself!" he whispered. "I don't know if you were entirely foolish or amazingly brave."

Looking into his eyes, she shook her head.

"I couldn't get into that plane. I just knew I couldn't!"

"Well, we can talk more later!" he murmured.

He didn't let her go, but he turned to the first man who came rushing from one of the cars that had burst onto the field, briefing him quickly on what had happened.

The man nodded, wanting to know if there was anyone else anywhere, and Chase told him that they hadn't seen a pilot and didn't know if anyone else was in the plane, but if so, they hadn't appeared.

Other agents were out of their cars, communicating in a way that Sky didn't understand. But two headed up the steps to the plane, one right behind the other, weapons drawn, ready for what they would encounter within.

Another car drove in.

It was Wellington himself who jumped out, rushing

over to them. He looked anxiously from Sky to Chase, frowning.

"You got Malcolm—and *Miguel Esposito*?" he exclaimed.

"I had some help," Chase said, managing a grin. "A really great dog—and then a true heroine not about to go anywhere quietly."

Wellington frowned, once again looking from Chase to Sky.

"And Larry. Hmm. They may want that dog back," Wellington said.

"They're not getting him!" Sky said, smiling. Her eyes fell on Malcolm and then Esposito, and she shivered and looked away.

She was so grateful to be alive.

And still…she wanted to be away from the blood and the horror and the fear.

"It will all be in my report," Chase said, "but there's something I never knew about Sky. She's got one hell of a kick and a tremendous sense of balance. It helped that Esposito ducked back into the plane at the right moment and Sky had made a dive to safety. But—"

"Sir!"

One of the agents who had gone into the plane reappeared.

"Yes, Cooper. Empty?"

"No, sir. Just a terrified woman who doesn't speak English. My Spanish isn't great, but I think that she was kidnapped and forced to act as a server on the plane and—and I'm not sure what else. She was hiding on the floor in the galley."

Wellington nodded. "We'll get her some help and figure out her situation. Can you talk her down so we can bring her in?"

The agent nodded. The woman emerged, looking at them terrified. Then she saw Esposito's body, fallen to the tarmac.

She let out a cry, but it wasn't a cry of loss or pain.

It was one of relief. Shaking, she turned into the arms of the agent who had to catch her before she, too, became a casualty of the short flight of steps.

"It's okay, you're okay, you're going to be okay!" the agent reassured her.

He helped her down, and as he escorted her to one of the vehicles, she looked over at Chase and Sky and suddenly broke away, running to hug Sky, speaking so quickly.

Sky, knocked a foot away from Chase, thought that the poor woman had been a victim—like so many others. Kidnapped? Maybe members of her family had been threatened, too.

Larry was amazing; he didn't growl. He knew the woman was no threat. The shepherd/Lab mix sensed her fear and trauma and leaned his furry body next to both her and Sky.

Sky wasn't sure what to do, but she hugged the woman back, smoothing her hair and telling her that it was going to be okay.

The woman broke away at last, hugged Chase and then hurried to join the agent.

"We'll find out more about her," Wellington said, looking at Sky and smiling. "Maybe you should be on our payroll."

She smiled and shook her head. "Um… I think I'll stick to teaching kids."

"Far more dangerous!" Wellington said lightly. He hesitated. "We're going to need a debriefing on all this, of course. And Sky, I'm sorry, I hope you're feeling up to—"

"I'm here. I'm alive. And I'm up to anything needed," she said. "But, please, do you know anything more about Chris and the other man?"

"In surgery as we speak, but the prognosis on both is good," Wellington told her. "So I'm afraid that there are a few things that still need attention..."

Chase was smiling at her. "She is the bravest individual I know," he said. "And we'll be fine. Paperwork. It comes with everything."

Medical techs had arrived; gurneys were coming out. Forensic crews were heading onto the plane.

"You are something!" Chase told her very softly. He hesitated. "You are your father's daughter."

"And that," she told him, "is the greatest compliment I could receive. Thank you. And thank you—and Larry. You saved my life."

"You saved your own life. And Larry played his part, distracting Esposito after Malcolm was down."

She hugged the dog again. "And to think I didn't even know I needed a dog! But Larry, I promise you the best treats forever and ever."

She saw Chase smiling slightly and turned to him. "Do I get the best treats forever, too?" he asked.

"Yeah. This time, forever—and ever!" she promised.

Chapter Eleven

The night was long.

"Worst part of the job," Chase teased as they sat at headquarters. He had to speak lightly. He was afraid that if he didn't, if he thought of the way it might have all ended, he'd cease being rational.

He thought about Sky, about meeting as kids…friends. Friends who came together again when they were of age, friends who fell in love then, and…

Maybe there were such things as soulmates. He hadn't lived like a monk, but in the years between he'd just never fallen in love. He'd had relationships, but…

Nothing right.

Then, when it seemed that pretend might turn to reality—or might have been real all along whether that had been admitted or not—he might have lost her.

Forever.

"Hey!"

Sky touched his arm. It was morning; there really hadn't been a night. But despite her worry that they bring Larry back home and give him the assurances he needed, she'd insisted that they get to the hospital.

Miraculously, while several agents had been injured, none had been killed.

And Chris Wiley was going to be fine.

When they arrived at the hospital, Chase told Sky, "We're going to have to see Hank quickly before anyone else. He won't believe that *you* are okay if he doesn't see you himself. We'll be brief because I know—"

"I'm happy to see Hank and then Chris," she replied.

"And we'll check in on Bobby Sacks, too. Bobby was a hell of a help in this."

"Oh, did they find out anything about the woman—"

"Alina Gomez. She's fine. Wellington is going to help get her asylum status. Esposito's goons killed her father for refusing to distribute his goods at a school. Then, he just swept up Alina as his personal property. She's going to be fine," he reiterated.

She smiled. "Okay, onward to Hank and then Chris!"

Chase's grandfather was awake when they entered the room.

"About time!" he boomed. "Thankfully, I didn't know about most of this until it was over. You two…you know, you did good. You did really good. But don't do it again! You scared the bejesus out of me!"

Chase and Sky both gave him hugs, and Hank told them that he'd be transferring into rehab the next day, and that by the end of the month…

"I'll be drumming my heart out again! And you!" he said, wagging a finger at Chase.

"Gramps, I—"

"I'm not suggesting that you quit anything. You don't have to worry. The news is filled with the whole event, but a lot is focused on you—not as an agent, Chase, but just as the drummer who went after his beloved. The word is out there that supposedly law enforcement brought down a major drug ring and just that you…you're a hot drummer and lover. And you, Miss Ferguson! Like a new age Disney princess, kicking ass!"

"Um, thanks," Sky murmured.

"Your dad…well, you know what I believe? I believe he was looking out for you from the clouds, and that… My God, girl, he would be so proud. No, I believe we'll meet again. He is proud. And your mother—"

Sky let out a squeak. "Oh, my God! I haven't called my mother, and she'll see the news!"

"Maybe you should do that," Hank said.

The look Sky gave Chase was a little panicked. He smiled and told her, "Step out, give her a ring. Make sure she knows that you didn't get so much as a bruise from the whole thing."

Sky nodded and went out into the hall.

Hank watched her leave and turned to Chase.

"Don't let her get away this time," he said.

"Well, I didn't mean to let her get away *last* time."

"Make it permanent, then," Hank said.

"Gramps, I can't force her into something. These have been the most intense days of my life, but we've just gotten together again—"

"I don't think that either of you were ever really apart. You know, I remember when Jake fell in love with Mandy. There had never been anyone he loved like her before in his life, and he knew that there never would be again."

"I know that Sky is all that to me," Chase told him. "But I can't make her—"

"Marry you?"

He turned. Sky was back in the room, grinning and looking relieved as she walked in.

He ignored the question first, asking her anxiously, "Your mom?"

"Oh, she's mad at me, but she says that she's way more relieved than angry. And she's coming home from Ireland. I told her the events were over…but she's coming home."

"That's great! I look forward to seeing her," Hank said. "Now, as to the other. This big, brave undercover agent is afraid to ask you to marry him."

"Gramps!" Chase protested.

But Skylar turned to him, grinning. "Yes, of course."

"Pardon?"

"Oh, come on. Don't make your grandfather do everything! Yes, I think we should definitely get married. I don't want a crazy wedding. I want our families. And Skyhawk. Oh, wait. Skyhawk is kind of my father's other kid, so that's family, too."

He looked at her. He'd loved her forever. And maybe that was why time had slipped away, and why time, now, was everything.

They weren't going to waste any more of it.

But two could play the game.

"Sure," he said. "I'll marry you."

They both laughed. And it was, in truth, nice that right there, in his grandfather's hospital room, he drew her into his arms for a kiss that was a promise for a lifetime.

"Okay, okay, get a room!" Hank said, shaking his head. "Oh, yeah, you have rooms. Nope, you have houses. So…"

"We still need to see Chris, and I want to check on Bobby Sacks," Chase told him.

"Then, go do it. You can stop by tomorrow afternoon and see me here. Rehab place after that, and I'll be working hard, I promise. I'm not handing over my drum set entirely yet!"

"You better not do that," Chase warned him. "I'm not ready. All this is..."

"It's a lot," Hank agreed. "All this tonight...and I was here. Well, thankfully, they're going to let me see Chris soon. Maybe now! Hey, ring the nurse. See if you can walk me into his room."

"They'll want you in a wheelchair," Chase said.

"They can put me in a rocket ship if they want. I'd just really like to see my old friend."

"I'm on it," Sky said, hurrying out.

In a minute she was back with a wheelchair—and a nurse. The nurse saw to it that her charge was safely seated.

"Now, please, this isn't at all regular... You shouldn't even be visiting at this hour, but keep the noise level down. It's just five a.m., and the patients need their rest!"

"Yes, ma'am!" Chris promised.

"Well, good to see you all. Mr. Wiley needs to sleep, but he's too worried about events and Miss Ferguson and... please. Go in."

They entered, and Sky hurried to Chris's side, taking his hand.

As she did so, Chase noticed that Brandon was asleep in a chair by the window.

And Mark Reynolds was there, too, standing now, though he'd been seated in a chair by the bed. Chase realized that Joe Garcia was also in Chris's room and he smiled, surprised that the hospital had turned a blind eye to so many visitors.

Especially at this hour, as the nurse had pointed out. But they were there.

Skyhawk was there. The old group, friends before they'd been a band. All—thankfully—innocent of the machinations and terror going on around them.

Chris looked up at Sky, smiled and squeezed her hand.

"I was so worried!" Sky told him.

"We all were," Mark Reynolds said quietly. "Worried about you, too—crazy worried about you."

"I'm fine, I'm fine. It was Chris who was shot!" Sky said.

"Chris, what did they tell you? I mean, you were in surgery—" Chase began.

"Funny thing is, the guy played so many people—but he was a lousy shot," Chris said. "Caught me below the bone, didn't even shatter anything. They got the bullet out, they sewed me up, and I'm just about as good as can be."

"Hey, Chris is tough!" Joe said.

Brandon had woken up, and he blinked and stood, coming over to the bed. "Dad! You are not good as new. You're going to behave. You were warned that the big fear is going to be infection, and you'll have to be careful—"

"I will!" Chris argued. "You're the wild child."

"Not so much anymore, trust me," Brandon said, looking around at all of them. His eyes fell on Sky. "And you!" he said softly, turning to Chase. "She walked out with Malcolm, you know, because he threatened to kill me."

"But it all worked out!" Sky said.

"How the hell?" Brandon asked.

"Teamwork!" Chase said. "Sky kicked ass, Larry distracted the one guy, and..."

"You brought 'em down," Brandon finished. "It's been

all over the news. Right now, a lot of confusion. Apparently, reporters know that Esposito was running a major drug-distribution ring through several venues. Working with people like Malcolm—threatening families, little children—to get what they wanted done. Right now, they're just saying that members of Skyhawk were injured, but that—hmm, how did they put it, Dad?"

"They said that members of Skyhawk held their own and helped bring down a crew of major criminals. People knew you were kidnapped, Sky, and they knew that Chase came after you—I think they even knew a dog was involved, but the reporters have been shockingly careful about what they're reporting. Still…"

"Still, there's going to be enough publicity to make us all crazy…and rise to the top of the charts!" Mark said. He shook his head. "But that's not what matters. I'm just grateful, so incredibly grateful, that we're all here. That Chris is going to be okay, that Hank is on the mend. That Sky and Chase—"

"And Larry!"

"And Larry? Okay, the thing is, we made it. And we know the truth behind what happened to Jake, all those years ago, Jake meant to get it all torn down. And… Chase, Sky, you knew. The rest of us were devastated but never saw it as anything other than an accident. We always knew that Jake was best, and thanks to him, we all know how to be our best, and thanks to you, Sky, and you, Chase, we've all survived—and lots of people will live. All is good. Hey, I could pass out some Jell-O and we could all toast one another?" Mark finished.

They all laughed softly.

"Think I'll pass on the hospital Jell-O," Chase told

them. "And I want to go and check on Bobby quickly. If they'll let me, of course."

"I think they'll let you do just about anything tonight—or this morning," Hank asserted.

Chase nodded. He glanced at Sky and smiled and slipped out into the quiet hall. He spoke briefly to the police officer on duty, who assured him that he was welcome to look in on Bobby Sacks, though the patient might be sleeping.

But when Chase stepped silently into the room, Bobby's eyes were open.

"I'd hoped you'd stop by to see me!" Bobby said. "I… oh, man, I've got to admit, after I talked to you, I was pretty terrified. Because there were layers to what was going on, people who did know who the players were, people who didn't…and everyone worried about their loved ones if they didn't follow through. But…is the news real? They say the FBI brought down the kingpin, but they say that they followed you, that you were involved."

"I think it's safe, Bobby. And I just wanted to say I know that you were scared to say anything. You did. You talked, even terrified. So you were a help, just as much as anyone."

Bobby smiled. "That's great news. I have other great news."

"That's great. Really great!"

Bobby's smile deepened. "I'm going to live! No permanent damage to my major organs. Somehow… Well, you really saved my life. I owe it to you."

"No. You owe a good life to yourself," Chase told him. He patted Bobby's shoulder. "Just stick with it, keep getting better and better. And right now, I'm going to leave you before they throw me out."

Bobby nodded. "Thank you!"

Chase nodded and waved, leaving Bobby's room and heading back to Chris's.

The nurse met him in the hall.

"There are sick people in this hospital, Mr. McCoy. Now, I am aware it was a difficult night for you all, but you've seen your friends and your grandfather, and now it's time for you to leave," she informed him.

He smiled. "Yes, ma'am. We'll be getting right out of here," he promised.

Stepping back into Chris's room, he saw that everyone in the room seemed comfortable and relaxed. His grandfather sat in his wheelchair, Chris was in his bed, Joe was on the chair in the corner with Brandon perched on the edge of it, Mark was still standing by the bed, and Skylar was seated at the foot of it.

They all looked up when he came in.

"Bobby Sacks?" Mark asked.

"Pulling through fine, too," Chase informed them. "But we've just been thrown out. Hank, we need to wheel you back, and the rest of us—"

"Need to go. Right. But we'll see you in the morning," Brandon promised his father.

"It is morning!" Chris reminded him. "Go home, all of you. Adrenaline has run out. You had a great show—and then all hell broke loose. Go!"

"Wait!" Hank said. "Someone has an announcement for us."

Hank stared at him hard.

"Oh! Yes, we do—"

"But we don't have a date, we want to see my mom—" Sky began.

"Oh, my God, took you two long enough!" Brandon exclaimed. "Wow, and yay!"

"Legacy," Mark said, looking around the room. "Chase, Sky, beautiful. We couldn't be happier for you. We'll have to hire a band for the wedding because—"

"Because we hope you'll all be celebrating with us!" Sky said.

"Because the lead singer will be a bit busy," Joe said, laughing. "Seriously, guys, we couldn't be happier. And I know that…somewhere…"

"My dad is happy and proud," Sky finished.

"So before the demon nurse gets back," Chris said jokingly, "we should probably clear out. You have to roll me back to my own room, and then—"

Apparently, the group did still think alike. It was almost as if they'd planned it, rehearsed.

Chris, Mark, Joe, Hank and Brandon all shouted, "Get a room!"

LARRY. LARRY WAS the best dog ever, Sky was convinced.

When they reached her house, her first move was to drop down by the dog and embrace him, scratching and petting him, telling him just how much she loved him.

Larry, of course, lapped it up.

Chase hunkered down by her, stroking the dog as well.

She looked at him. "Hmm. Trey Montgomery was a lecturer turned dog rescuer and trainer?"

Chase shrugged. "Trey spent thirtysomething years of his life working with the police canine division. He worked with all manner of disciplines—drug dogs, cadaver dogs, missing-persons dogs—and he had several of his own that could do just about anything." He hesitated. "I told him that—that I needed a dog for a very good and loving person who seldom thought about her own danger. Larry had taken a few bullets, and like any good cop, he was rewarded with retirement. But…"

"In the middle of all that happened, you thought to come back for him," Sky said.

"I was afraid I might have followed you into the bayou or a forest or… I didn't know. But I knew that if it was necessary, Larry could follow your trail. As it happened, we didn't need to find you. But everything was on split-second timing, and Larry bought us what we needed." He hesitated. "I was so afraid that if…"

"That if you hadn't gotten there when you did, Malcolm or Esposito would have shot me?" she asked, smiling. "Well, my plan was to knock him down and get his gun and hope that I could fire it," she informed him. "I mean, I did have a plan. I knew I wasn't just getting on that plane. But…"

"But?"

She smiled. "You did come."

He leaned over, delicately kissing her lips. "How did we let the years go by?" he whispered.

She shook her head. "It was my fault."

"No. There is no fault. Sky, I couldn't put the past to rest, either. And Wellington is an amazing man, brilliant at what he does. He believed in me—which was important. Of course, there were also a number of bad things happening around the state. They'll still be trying to clean it all up, but that's going to be for other agents. Hey, no one does this job alone, trust me."

"And yet you've managed to keep it secret—undercover you!"

He shrugged. "No one expects a guy born with a silver spoon in his mouth to run around really working."

Sky smiled and nodded. "Are we really getting married?"

He adjusted to be on his knees, dodging one of Larry's paws as the dog rolled over, expecting a belly rub.

"Larry, wait your turn!" Chase said. Then he turned to Sky. "Skylar Ferguson, it would be the greatest honor of my life if you would marry me. Um… I'm supposed to have a diamond. I'll take care of that—"

"I don't really care about the jewelry," she assured him. "You gave me a few amazing gifts already."

"Oh?"

"Well, Larry for one."

"Larry is cool. I grant you that."

"And in truth, you gave me my life."

"No, kid. You are your father's daughter. You had everything to do with saving your own life."

"Okay, then…you're giving me something I value as much."

"What's that?"

"You're putting *your* life in my hands!"

He leaned over the dog, taking Sky into his arms, kissing her long and deeply with all the emotion from the depths of his heart.

Larry let out a little disgruntled moan of protest, and they broke apart, laughing.

"I'll see to Larry's bowls and all," Chase said.

"I'll start the shower."

"Yeah, shower, that will be good."

"All touch of monsters gone!" she told him.

And that was it. They scrambled up, Chase heading for the kitchen, Sky streaking up the stairs. She realized how much had happened, and all in the last sixteen hours or so.

And now…

She wanted a good, hot spray. Lots of heat and tons of mist. She stepped in ahead of Chase, glad to have the heat, to feel renewed from all that had gone on.

She'd been so close to…

Death.

But now life loomed ahead of her. She had been right: she and Chase—with the help of agents, police and friends—had proven the truth of the man her father had been, never careless, always clean, always caring about others.

And even before that…

She had realized what she had thrown away. But Chase had never forgotten. Never really left her. And now they had a chance.

He slipped in behind her. She felt the heat of his body, deeper, more encompassing than any other. She turned into his arms, and with the water sluicing over them they kissed and touched and scrubbed. They managed to laugh as the soap slipped to the tub bottom, as they both reached for it, crashing into one another, nearly falling, catching each other…touching and kissing again.

Then they were out, so they wouldn't fall, drying, laughing…

Making their way back to the bedroom.

Making love.

She had no clue how many hours passed, but at one point, she rolled over, half-asleep, and noticed that there was a gun on the bedside table, not the one he'd had earlier—

He noticed her curiosity.

"A service weapon is always taken when it's been fired under such circumstances," he told her. "They'll return my regular one."

"And that—"

"Is a personal backup. I think… I think it's over. But like it or not, fame follows what we've done and…"

"You went into what you do because you knew that something had happened and happened very wrong," Sky said seriously, looking into his eyes. "I don't know everything you've done through the years, but I know it's been important to you."

"I—I can stop."

She shook her head. "No, Chase. You're the man I love. And you're the man I love because of all your determination, because you do want… Well, none of us can fix the world, but you want to do what you can to stop very bad things. I don't want you to change."

He ran his fingers gently through her hair, shaking his head. "You are amazing. And you—"

"I love what I do. I'm not always sure I'm changing the world, but I love kids. I love working with them, and I always hope that I've given them something that they can love, that they can do, that can keep them from… other things."

He nodded. "I love kids, too. We are having a few, right?"

"Five or six."

"What?"

She laughed. "One at a time, and we'll see how it goes."

"Legacy!" he teased.

"Legacy. So…"

"We don't have to be anywhere at all today. We can just..."

"All right!"

She rolled back into his arms.

A while later, they finally slept. And it was night when they woke up, ran down to take Larry out and dig around in the kitchen.

And then, of course, they realized that they had dozens of missed phone calls, and that while the night of both amazement and horror was over, other things might be just beginning.

But that was okay.

Because now they both knew they had a lifetime together.

Epilogue

The events at the arena had naturally created a media sensation. While Sky would rather have been kept out of everything, there were too many people who had been involved, and the coverage went on for weeks.

And, in due time, Mandy Ferguson returned from Ireland, a pile of mixed emotions. She had been terrified for her only child, and then, of course, grateful.

She didn't seem the least surprised that Sky and Chase were together again.

"Honey, honey, you are the best daughter, loving your dad so much!" she told Sky as she hugged her repeatedly. "I mean…who knew we were waiting for this, but…"

Unsurprisingly, Sky was wanted for interviews. At first, she'd wanted nothing to do with them. And then she realized that she didn't want to be seen as a pathetic victim, but when he'd talked to the press, Chase had let them all know that she'd been instrumental in saving her own life.

And she was grateful—grateful, too, that was Chase just being… Chase.

More than anything else, she wanted the world to know that they were all lucky, that all law enforcement involved had been exemplary, and that it had been a far-reaching thing.

And even now, years after his death, they could be grateful to her father: he'd been the one to first realize what had been going on, and it had been the knowledge that he would never have let it go on that had gotten him killed.

Amazingly, Chase being undercover was never revealed. He had just so happened to be the drummer that night.

And in interviews, he would just smile and remind the world that he'd acted like any man in love—he'd gone to find his fiancée.

In the midst of it all, Hank McCoy was let out of the hospital. The rehab he was going to be at for the next several weeks was in Arizona and, as much as she loved her home state, Sky was ready to leave it for a while.

Mandy suggested that they all head to Arizona for a while, find a quiet place and let things settle down.

Sky wasn't so sure; she made her own schedule. Chase didn't.

But Wellington came through. At Sky's house, visiting the happy couple, getting to know Mandy, he assured Chase that a vacation was going to be something that he both needed and deserved.

And so they headed out to Arizona to spend some time simply getting away.

They planned a small wedding because Sky really wanted it to be special with just the guests they knew and loved in attendance. They would head to her favorite church in New Orleans, and the service itself would be part of Jazz Mass.

Their reception would be small as well. They would have it at home.

Something else happened while they were in Arizona.

A second romance bloomed.

Chris's wife had been gone many years.

And at first…

It just seemed like two old friends spending time together, making the days go by. Mandy was in good health—always grateful for it, she often assured Sky—and she was very happy to be there and help Chris through his rehab.

Wonderful.

They were often together working while Sky and Chase headed off to the OK Corral, a museum, Sedona, or…

Just off alone!

But when Chris had finished his rehab and they were all seated in the little house they had rented for the stay, Mandy said seriously that she had something to tell them.

They gathered around the kitchen table.

Mandy lowered her head. "We're going to be m—"

Sky glanced at Chase, frowning, and Chase glanced back at her.

"What's happened? Has something happened, suggested that anything bad is going to happen? M—murdered?"

Mandy looked up at them. "Married! We're going to be married. I'm sorry. I mean, we never want to upset you kids and, Sky, I know how you felt—"

Sky couldn't help it. She broke out into relieved laughter.

"Mom! The one thing I know for sure about Dad is how much he loved you—and he loved Chris, too. If I know anything at all about my father, he'd want you both to be happy!"

Her mom jumped up and ran around to hug her.

They all wound up standing. Hugging. Laughing and happy.

"But," Sky said, "no double wedding!"

Mandy laughed. "We're running off to Vegas."

"That'll work," Chase assured them.

"Well, we mean today!"

"Go for it!" Sky said.

And so, Mandy and Chris went on to Vegas, and Sky and Chase returned home. And in another month, they had the small but beautiful wedding she had wanted, and even though she loved every minute of it, the wedding itself hadn't mattered.

Making something wonderfully real on paper that already lived in her heart and soul did. And, of course, at the house for the reception…

They didn't hire another band. They wound up jamming…

And when Mark Reynolds asked her what the future would bring, she assured him, "Chase and I have to live our own lives, but we will be around!"

She lifted her glass and said, "Skyhawk forever!"

Her words were echoed by the group.

Chase slipped around behind her, pulling her tight.

"*Sky-lar and Chase forever*!"

She smiled, leaning against him.

"Sky-lar and Chase. Forever and ever and ever!"

And she knew that it would be so.

* * * * *